What this Book Does

English-speaking children in India have little access to good writing in Indian languages. So we decided to begin a series called *Translations from Indian Languages,* starting with Bengali. Children's writing in Bengali goes back to the late nineteenth century. It is vibrant and humorous, consisting of detective fiction, nonsense verse, ghost stories, fantasy and science fiction.

In India adults usually want moralistic tales for children. Such stories re-inforce established and often unexamined ideas. We think literature has wider functions, one of which is to open new worlds for the reader to delight in. We don't have enough available original Indian writing of this kind in English, so that our children grow up with literature which suggests that fun and excitement invariably happen in contexts other than their own.

We have chosen to publish *Four Heroes and a Haunted House* precisely because it is non-didactic. A whimsical book which plays with the form of the detective novel, it also invites the reader to savour the oddities of language - of puns, idiosyncratic metaphors, and absurd turns-of-phrase.

The design of the book reflects this quirkiness, in the way the chapter titles and page numbers break out of regularity. We decided against illustrating the novel and limiting the imaginative absurdities of the text.

Four Heroes and a Haunted House

© Tara Publishing, 1998

Narayan Gangopadhyay

Translation	Swati Bhattacharjee
Design	Rathna Ramanathan
Production	C. Arumugam, Radhika Raviprakash
Printer	The Ind-Com Press, Chennai

Tara Publishing

20/GA Shoreham, 5th Avenue

Besant Nagar, Chennai 600 090

Distribution

Goodbooks Pvt. Ltd.

7 Prithvi Avenue

Chennai 600 004

ISBN 81-86211-34-9

Narayan Gangopadhyay

contents

Uncle's Roar of Laughter

The school leaving exam was over.

Sitting on the verandah of the Chatterjees' home, the three of us were chatting happily–Chairman Teni, Habul Sen and I. I am Pyalaram Banerjee. I stay in Patoldanga and have only fish stew for lunch. Kyabla, our fourth member, was yet to come.

All four of us had sat for the exams. Kyabla was the brightest among us–the headmaster had said he might get a scholarship. Habul Sen of Dhaka was also likely to get a first division. As for me, I have already been stumped twice in maths. This time, I might just get a third division.

And as for Teni...

The less said about Teni, the better. He sat in the tenth standard like a monument, year after year. No one could move him even an inch from his seat there. But Teni did not mind. "Heh heh," he would say, "Shouldn't we have one or two old hands in the class? I mean, those who know things. After all, someone must 'manage' the new boys."

The new boys were being 'managed' all right. Even Teni's eldest brother, the very sound of whose voice always made us run, had been nearly 'managed'. Three, four years ago, every time Teni failed, he fretted, fumed and created a scene. "How many ounces of cowdung does that Teni have in his head?" he wondered aloud. Now, even he had stopped bothering. So used had he become to Teni failing his exams, that if Teni suddenly cleared them, he would surely faint straight away.

So we were happily chatting.

That idiot Habul raised the topic of exams. Teni at once screwed up his nose and said, "Shut up, will you? All those foolish exams! A handful of stupid boys cram a whole lot of books and pass tests. What's so great about that? What is really difficult is not to pass. Look at me: year after year I sit in the exam hall, answer all the questions in all the papers, yet no examiner can ever make me pass. That is real credit."

"You're right, Tenida," I said. "That's why I am follow-ing your great example. My uncle pulls my ears so hard that they have become longer, but I am not one to betray my school! Haven't I hung on for two years?"

"Don't you dare speak, Pyala," Teni said. "I had hoped you would make an able disciple. But even you have betrayed me! How could you answer thirty-six marks correct in the maths paper? And even if you did, why didn't you cancel the sums?"

"I am really sorry!" I said, scratching my neck shamefacedly.

"The world is full of betrayers," grumbled Teni. "Anyway, forget it. Now tell me, what are we planning to do in the holidays? Are we going to sit right here in Calcutta, doing nothing? Shouldn't we go for a trip somewhere?"

I was delighted. "Oh yes, let's go! My aunt stays in Liluah, a little way from Howrah. We can have a lovely time at her place..."

"Pyala, you idiot, will you shut up?" Teni made a face at me. "Your ears are like a goat's, and so are your ideas. Liluah! What a place to suggest! Why not the Hatibagan Market? Or the roof of your house? Just my luck to have friends with weak stomachs and weaker brains."

Habul Sen thought hard. "What about Burdwan?" he said, in his East Bengal accent. "My uncle is the D.S.P of police there..."

"What? That remote town?" Teni screwed up his nose again. "Once one boards a train, one can't help landing up in Burdwan. I mean, all trains seem to go to Burdwan. And all the way, the jhug-jhug of the engine, the jam-packed plat-forms! But still…''. Teni scratched the top of his head once. "You get good sweets there–*sitabhog, mihidana*. We might think about it. At least it is better than Liluah!"

What an insult! Teni was insulting my aunt's house! I lost my temper. "Oh yes, Burdwan is surely better," I quipped. "Only, the mosquitoes there are about the size of sparrows. If a few of them get into your mosquito net at night, they will make sitabhog and mihidana out of you! Besides, Habul's uncle is the D.S.P there, you heard yourself! If you start a fight with anyone, Tenida, Uncle will surely throw you into the lockup in no time!"

That put out Teni a little. "Don't talk rot," he said. "Hey Habul, how's your uncle?"

Habul thought a bit. "Pyala is not very wrong," he said. "My uncle was in the military, he has a real military temper!"

"Then why on earth should we visit such dangerous uncles?" Teni grumbled. "Really Habul, I don't know what to do with you."

Our discussion had got this far, when Kyabla suddenly appeared like a gust of wind, a plate of *alu chaat* in his hands.

"Hey, here's Kyabla," said Teni, jumping up–and in a second the alu chaat had changed hands. Teni put nearly half of it in his mouth in one go. "Mmm, wonderful! Where did you get this Kyabla?"

Kyabla replied cheerfully, "A man is selling it near the main road."

"Is he still there? Why don't you get us some more?"

"Why, only alu chaat?" said Kyabla. "Why not *pulao*, chicken, prawn cutlet, pineapple chutney, sweets..."

"Ish...sh," Teni drew a long breath. "Stop Kyabla, please stop! All those names on an empty stomach! I will surely have a heart attack."

"If you do, you'll be sorry, Tenida," laughed Kyabla. "All those dishes are being cooked in our house today. And Ma asked me to invite all three of you."

For full three minutes, we stared open-mouthed. Then Teni jumped up. "Really, Kyabla, really? You're not joking?"

"Why should I? My uncle has come from Ranchi. He himself went to the market to buy all the goodies."

"And chicken? Are you sure there's chicken? Come on Kyabla, I am a Brahmin, remember! If you let me down, you'll surely be reborn as a chicken!"

"Don't worry. I saw half-a-dozen chickens tied to our verandah, raising a racket."

"Trim, trim, tra-la-la-la...", Teni started to hum and dance. The three of us joined in the chorus. A stray dog was startled. It let out a howl and ran, its tail between its legs.

How can I describe the dinner? The way Teni ate, we thought we would need a crane to lift him up. He downed a kilo of meat, a dozen cutlets–and still kept eating. I wondered whether he would chew up the plates too!

But Kyabla's uncle was such fun! We had him with us during dinner. And what stories he told us! When he described how he once gripped the tail of a wild buffalo and made it go round and round, we laughed till we thought we would burst!

On another hunting trip, he said, the branch on which he was sitting snapped, and he landed right on a tiger's back. Did the tiger eat him up? Far from it–the animal fainted right away! He must have thought a demon had caught hold of him. Even when he was put into a cage, the tiger did not wake up. Only after he was given smelling salts and sprinkled with water did the tiger come back to his senses!

Uncle told us more stories after dinner. We sat on the terrace. Uncle lay on an easy chair, smoking one cigarette after another, while we sat on a mat listening to him. Moonlight played on Uncle's bald pate. His face looked strange in the reddish light of his lit cigarette.

"So you want to go on a trip?" said Uncle. "I can suggest a place. You won't find such a beautiful and healthy place so close to here."

"Ranchi?" asked Kyabla.

"No, no, it's too hot in Ranchi. Besides it's too crowded."

"Darjeeling? Or Shillong, perhaps?" said Teni.

"Too cold," replied Uncle. "It's painful to roast in the heat, but there is no fun if you freeze with cold either. No, none of these places."

I felt I had to say something. "What about Gobardanga?"

"Shut up, Pyala. Shut up I say!" Teni was furious. "Can't you think of anything better than Liluah and Gobardanga?"

"Quiet, quiet," said Uncle. "No one in Calcutta has yet heard of this place I am talking about. It is close to Ranchi and you can go there from Hazaribagh and Ramgarh. After a bus journey, you have to go about six miles by a bullock cart.

It's a beautiful place—*saal* and *mahua* forests all around, a lake with clear, cool water. You can see deer in daylight, rabbits and wild pheasants. There is a Santhal village close by, you can get milk and meat real cheap from them. There's also some fish from the lake—two or four paisa a kilo. There I have bought a nice bungalow on the top of a small hill. The sahib who built it sold it to me before he went back to England.

It's a wonderful place! You can sit in the verandah and look on to the horizon. There is a stream right next to the bungalow, with water all round the year. If you stay there for a month—from the bag of bones that you are, you will come back with a body like that of Bhim Bhavani, the famous wrestler."

Teni had been reclining on a cushion. Now he sat up. "We will go. All four of us!"

Uncle lit another cigarette. "I'm glad to hear that. But there's a problem."

"What?"

"Er...well...the house is said to be haunted. The Santhals say demons sometimes walk in it, and someone cries out suddenly in the night. But nothing can be seen. I have gone there three times, but stayed only during the day. So I have no idea what happens at night. So I was wondering whether you all will dare to go down there."

"Phooh!" said Teni. "All that is rubbish. There is no such thing as a ghost. Four of us will go there, and if we catch sight of the ghost, we will send him straight to the mental hospital at Ranchi. Besides..."

But Teni could say no more. Suddenly he stopped and clasped Habul Sen tightly.

Habul jumped. "Ah, ah! What are you doing, Tenida? Let me go!"

But Teni wouldn't release him. He squeezed Habul even tighter and cried, "What's that? What's that on the roof?"

The moon had gone behind a small black cloud. All around us was a strange darkness. But, on the roof of the house next to ours, there gleamed a pair of strange non-human eyes.

Kyabla's uncle let out a tremendous laugh. My God, what a laugh! My ears started singing, my stomach began to churn. I felt as if all the chicken I had eaten would come out squawking.

I had never heard so loud, so strange a laugh in my life!

A Pot Full of Yogic Serpents

It was all too much for me! Kyabla's uncle's awful roar of laughter, and those two burning eyes next door on top of that. I was thinking, should I run for the stairs, when...

Miaow!

The owner of those two burning eyes jumped on the wall, and from there to the house next door.

Uncle stopped his demonic laugh and said, "You people nearly fainted at the sight of a tomcat. How can you think of going to the haunted bungalow?'" He laughed some more, making fun of us. "Heroes do not grow on trees," he said at last.

Among us, only Kyabla was not too scared. He replied, as if on cue, "No, they grow in Patoldanga, like *patols*."

Habul freed himself from Teni's grasp and said, panting, "Or may be like *jamuns*, on top of trees."

"Or like pumpkins, on rooftops," I had to add.

Teni was waiting to get his breath back. Now, he scowled and said, "Shut up, all of you, don't talk nonsense. Believe me, Uncle, I...er...wasn't afraid at all. I was just pulling Pyala's leg. He got such a scare, poor boy!"

So he wanted to pass the buck? I was angry. I made a face like a loony and said, "Not at all, Uncle. Tenida was about to faint, so I shouted, just to buck him up."

"Bucking me up, were you?" Teni screwed up his nose till his face looked like a pickled mango. "So you fancy you are a strongman? Look Pyala, if you try to act smart, I will give you such a slap that your ears will land at Aravalli!"

"Enough, enough. I can see how brave you are," said Uncle. "But let's get back to business. Do you really want to go to Jhanto Hills?"

Jhanto Hills? Where on earth was that?

"And why on earth should we go there?" said Teni.

"But we were just talking of that place!" said Uncle.

"Oh, oh," Teni scratched his head. "Is Jhanto Hills the name of the place? I didn't quite get that. But, well, I must say one can hardly call Jhanto a nice name."

"Yes, what a horrible name!" echoed Habul.

"Heh heh heh," laughed Uncle, making a nasty sound. "That means you are not going. Scared, aren't you?"

Teni sprang up, did a quick sit-up and said, "Fear? I don't know what fear is." He slapped his chest and declared, "If no one wants to go, I shall go alone!"

Kyabla asked, "And what if the ghosts of Jhanto Hills catch you?"

"Then I will make chutney out of the ghost and eat it up," cried Teni, brimming over with energy. "Really, I mean it, I shall go alone."

Suddenly I felt enthused. "I am coming!"

"Me too," said Kyabla.

Habul Sen of Dhaka cried, "I will come with you!"

Uncle asked, again, "Won't you feel scared?"

"Of course not!" Teni stuck out his chest.

I was about to say so too, when that idiot Kyabla quipped, "Unless he sees a tomcat at night!"

Uncle's laugh shook the roof once again. Teni roared, "Look Kyabla, if you start talking too much, one blow of my fist will send your nose to..."

"Nashik," I added.

"Right! Well said, Pyala," said Teni. And he slapped me so hard on my back that I cried out, "Ooh-hoo!"

Let me tell you about the next few events in a few words. If I try to explain how we got permission from our parents, this story will become another Mahabharat. But after three days, four of us, with four suitcases on our shoulders and four rolls of bedding in our arms, reached Howrah station.

The train was nearly empty. Who would go to Ranchi at the height of summer, unless he was mad? We got into an empty second class coach and unrolled our four beds.

Just as I was about to lie down, Teni called me. "Hey, Pyala."

"What now?"

"I am really hungry, you know. I feel as if there's a whole team of mice boxing in my stomach."

"What! Didn't you finish nearly thirty *puris* and a kilo of mutton just before you came? Where have those gone?"

"You have the ash-bug inside you, Tenida," said Habul.

"I think so too," sighed Teni. "It must be an ash-bug. Whatever enters my stomach becomes ash in no time." He gave a broad smile. "I am a descendent of the great Agastya Muni, after all. Whatever enters me–*batapi, ilwal*–is digested then and there. I am a Brahmin, you know."

"And the horse lays eggs," said Kyabla. "Where is your sacred thread?"

"The thread?" Teni swallowed. "You know, when I try scratching my back with it when it's hot, it just snaps. But anyway, does a true Brahmin need the sacred thread? I have the Brahmin's superpower. But what to do now? The mice inside my stomach have started playing *kho-kho.*"

"Act as the referee," advised Kyabla.

"What did you say, Kyabla?"

"Nothing, nothing," Kyabla replied, and lay down flat on his bed.

And now Habul chirped, "Give that belly a blow, Tenida, and ask it to shut up."

"Oh? Whose belly needs a blow? Yours?" Teni was about to jump up, his big fist clenched.

"Not mine, Pyala's," replied Habul quickly.

I sprang up onto a bunk. "Why should I get a blow? I don't need it, not at all," I cried.

"Either you get a blow, Pyala, or you get me something to eat. There, can't you see the vendors? *Puri-kachori*, oranges, chocolate, *dalmot.* Get all or at least one of them."

"But I can see only a bootblack coming this way," I said like an obedient boy. "Should I call him?"

"How dare you?"

Teni was about to pounce on me, and I was thinking of jumping out of the window, when...

Dong! dong! dong! went a bell. Bhooooon! went the engine, and the train started moving.

Just then the door opened and someone entered the compartment, with a huge, suspicious-looking earthen pot. At the same moment, someone threw something inside the coach. It landed right on Teni's neck. "Ahhhhh," cried out Teni.

He was about to shout "What do you think you're doing?" when he swallowed hard and fell silent. So did we.

The man who had entered the coach was enough to make anyone shut up. He was an enormous *sadhu*, his face almost hidden behind a jungle of beard. A string of fat *rudrakshas* hung round his neck, and he had a red *sindoor* mark on his forehead. On his feet, he wore *nagra* shoes with upturned ends.

The sadhu put down the suspicious-looking pot and said, "Don't worry, my child. That is only my bedding. My disciple had to throw it in because of the hurry. You are not hurt, I hope?"

"No *Baba*, not much," mumbled Teni. "I'm sure the pain will go away in only seven days."

But I was grateful to the sadhu. Teni had wanted to beat me up, and now serves him right!

The sadhu smiled. "Only a bedding and you are flat, my child? Once, a huge *Kabuliwala*, with his ten kilo bag of *hing,* fell on my neck from a bunk. Even that did not kill me. I had to stay in hospital only for a week. Such is the power of yoga!"

"Then you must be a *Mahapurush*, sir! Please let me touch your feet," said Teni, and dived at the sadhu's feet.

"I'm glad, very glad," said the sadhu. "May good sense dawn upon you, child. But who are you? Where are you going?"

"*Prabhu*, we are going to Ramgarh. I am Bhajahari Mukherjee, alias Teni. That is Pyalaram Banerjee, who has fever every other day and has a liver like a football. This is Habul Sen who donates huge sums to our Patoldanga Thunder Club, and that one is Kyabla Mitra. He stands first in all exams and invites us often to his house for pulao and mutton."

"Pulao, mutton! Well, well, well." It looked as if the sadhu's mouth was watering behind his beard. "Good, good."

"Baba, may we know which Mahapurush you are?" asked Habul with folded hands.

"My name? Swami Ghutghutananda!"

"Ghutghutananda! What a name!" whispered Kyabla.

"Kyabla, my son, does that scare you? Do you know what was the name of my guru? He was called Damaru-Dhakka-Pattananada. His guru was called Ucchanda-

Martanda-Kukkuta-Dimba-Bharjananda. And his guru was called..."

"Please, Prabhu Ghutghutananda! Don't say any more! I can hardly breathe," I had to cry from the bunk.

Ghutghutananda smiled a benign smile. "Oh, you are but a child. Not that I can blame you. When I heard the name of the guru fourth removed from mine, I had hiccups for two days. So the four of you are going to Ramgarh. I am going to Muri, and then to Ranchi. Now children, my yogic sleep is a bit deep. The train reaches Muri early in the morning. Will you please wake me up?"

"Don't you worry. We will wake you up at Ghatshila," Kyabla assured him.

"No, no, my child, not so early. Ghatshila would be midnight."

"What about Tatanagar?"

"It will still be night at Tatanagar. Muri will do."

"Okay, we will do that," said Teni. "Now you can lie down for your yogic slumber."

"So I can!" said Ghutghutananda, and looked around once. "But where can I lie down? The four of you have occupied the four seats below. If I climb on a bunk, my yogic sleep will be disturbed."

"Why should you sleep on a bunk, Swami?" said Teni. "Pyala will sleep on a bunk. Pyala loves bunks."

How unfair! I have never liked bunks, I always feel I will fall down.

"No I don't," I cried out. "I don't like sleeping on bunks at all."

Teni glared at me. "Look Pyala, do you want to joke with a sadhu? You will surely go to hell. Swami, make your bed in Pyala's place. Pyala can sleep wherever he cares."

Ghutghutananda blessed Teni. "May you live long, my child," he said, promptly putting my bedding on the bunk and unrolling his own in its place. I could only look on.

Before he lay down, he drew the suspicious-looking pot under his seat. Teni had been observing the pot for quite some time. Now he asked, "What is in the pot, Swami?"

Ghutghutananda jumped at the question. "In the pot? There are terrible things inside the pot, my child. Yogic serpents!"

"Yogic serpents? What are they?" asked Habul.

Ghutghutananda raised his eyebrows till they almost touched his forehead. "They are dangerous and extremely poisonous snakes. I have captured them by my yogic power. Now they eat only milk and bananas and sing *bhajans*."

"Snakes sing bhajans?" I couldn't help asking.

"Nothing is impossible in yoga, my child. But don't you dare go anywhere near those snakes. You don't have yogic power, so they will bite you in a second!"

"We will be extremely careful, sir," said Teni like a good boy.

Ghutghutananda looked at all of us once. His eyes appeared suspicious. "Yes, be very careful," he said. "Don't even look at the pot. So can I lie down now?"

"Of course!"

Within five minutes, Ghutghutananda's nose started singing. Lying on the bunk and being rocked by the train, I too fell asleep. Suddenly, a sharp jab woke me up. Teni was poking my ribs.

"Come down, you idiot, before the sadhu wakes up!"

I looked down and saw the pot of yogic serpents on Teni's bed, its cover off. Habul and Kyabla were taking out *rosogollas* and *ladikenis* and popping them into their mouths.

"Are you coming, or will you just look on? We will have to put back the pot when we have finished."

Teni didn't have to say anything more. I jumped down, and lifted two ladikenis at once.

"Wait, wait. Don't finish everything. Leave some for me," said Teni.

The train left Tatanagar. Swami Ghutghutananda's nose continued to sing.

We were finished with the pot in five minutes. Teni finished half of it, Habul and I managed the rest. Kyabla, the youngest among us, could eat just two ladikenis and started licking his fingers.

Even then Teni would not leave the pot. He lifted it to his mouth and drank the syrup as well. Then he screwed up his nose and said, "I swallowed several ants too. Some were alive. Will they bite my insides?"

"Oh yes, they might," said Habul.

"Let them, what do I care?" said Teni. "Once I had eaten a jamun with a wasp in it. If the wasp couldn't do anything, what can a few ants do?"

"If you want, Tenida, you can eat up the entire Sundarban with the tigers and all. Who can stop you?" sighed Kyabla, having finished licking his fingers.

Throughout all this, Swami Ghutghutananda's nose kept singing. His yogic nose sang 'ghrrr...ghsshhh.'

"And your pot is finishhhed," mimicked Teni. "How dare you throw that twelve kilo bedding on my back! My neck is throbbing even now. But we have taken sweet revenge, haven't we, Pyala?"

"Oh yes! Heartless revenge!" I said.

Teni carefully covered up the mouth of the empty pot. Then he lay down and said, "Well, I feel better now after all those sweets. Now we can go to sleep."

Habul and I agreed. Only Kyabla kept grumbling, "You people ate all the sweets. I didn't get anything."

"Stop talking, Kyabla," said Teni. "You are but a kid. Do you want to fall ill by eating too much? Now go to sleep."

I never knew when Kyabla fell asleep, but Teni was asleep in two minutes. The Swami's nose said, 'Ghrrr' and Teni's nose replied, 'Frrrr.' I don't how long the duet went on, for I too fell asleep while trying to drive away the small insects from my face.

God's Gift — A Banana Skin

Muri. Muri Junction.

I woke up with a start and found that it was dawn.
Kyabla was already up, sipping a cup of tea. Habul was
yawning, and looking at Swami Ghutghutananda with nerv-
ous eyes. But the Swamiji and Teni were still at their snoring
duet.

Kyabla poked Teni's ribs.

"Who...who is that?" mumbled Teni, and sat up.

Kyabla said, "The train has been standing at Muri
station for ten minutes. Won't you wake up the Swami?"

Teni looked at the empty pot, and then at the sleeping
Swami. "When will the train start?" he asked.

"Right now, it seems."

"We will wake him up only after the train starts moving," said Teni. "If we wake him up now and he sees the empty pot, can you guess what will happen? Instead of the rosogollas, he will make breakfast out of us."

Teni was about to say to say something more, but at that moment, we heard a shout from outside: "Prabhuji, in which coach are you sleeping your yogic sleep?"

Was that a shout? It was more like a clap of thunder. The whole station trembled with the sound. And Swami Ghutghutananda jumped up.

"Prabhuji, wake up. The train will start."

"Oh! It's my disciple, Gajeshwar!" said the Swami. He put his head out of the window and called, "Gajo! Gajeshwar, my child! Here I am."

The door of the coach opened with a jerk. And at the sight of the man who entered, I jumped back on the bunk immediately. Habul and Teni lay down on their seats. Only Kyabla couldn't do anything, but the cup of tea slipped from his hands and landed on the floor.

"Ooh! My feet, my poor feet! What rascals these children are! I told them to wake me up at Muri, and see what they have done now. I would have got carried over."

Gajeshwar gave us a look. The very sight of his eyes turned our blood to water. Beside Gajeshwar, even the huge Swami looked like a stick. His complexion was soot-black, his size like an elephant, his head was shaved with only a *shikha* hanging from the middle of it. Gajeshwar looked at us with his tiny eyes and said, "Boys are like that these days Prabhu, like apes from Kishkindhya. "Would Prabhuji like me to box their ears, one by one?"

If Gajeshwar boxes our ears, they will surely come off in his hands. The four of us were terrified, and huddled together like *jalebis*. But we were in luck, for just then the bell rang, 'ting, ting, ting'!

Gajeshwar started to hurry, "Prabhuji, come down, come down! The train is leaving! We will think of their ears later, let's hurry now, we don't have time..."

He lifted the box, the bedding, and even the Swami on his back and stepped down from the train. At once the whistle went off and the train started moving.

We were still stiff with fear. The vision of Gajeshwar's hand, huge like an elephant's trunk, was dancing before our eyes. We had escaped by the skin of our teeth.

But no! As soon as the train had moved a few paces, Swamiji cried out, "My pot! My pot of rosogollas!"

Teni held up the pot and said, "No, no, not rosogollas, Prabhuji, your yogic serpents. Here they are!" And he threw the pot on the platform.

"Aaaah!" cried Swamiji and started running–and then he stopped. The pot had broken into a thousand pieces. But not even half a rosogolla was in it, or even a bit of a ladikeni!

"Prabhu, all your yogic serpents have escaped!" I said. I had nothing to fear now.

But oh! oh! What was that? Gajeshwar started chasing the train, running on his elephantine legs. His tiny eyes were spewing fire. Why, he was running faster than the train, he was about to jump into the coach...

I was ready to climb on the bunk again, Teni was getting ready to run towards the bathroom when...

God's gift–a banana skin!

Sss...rrr! went Gajeshwar and landed on his back on the platform. It wasn't just a slip, it was a Grand Fall!

"He is gone! Gone!" rose a cry. But Gajeshwar did not go anywhere. He was down for only five seconds. Then, limping, he stood up.

"We will meet again!" came his roar.

The train ran on full speed. Teni let out a deep sigh and said, "God is good!"

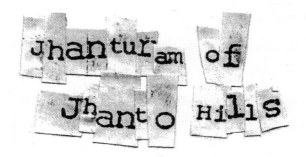

Jhanturam of Jhanto Hills

Nothing much happened on the way. We had a good laugh over Gajeshwar's Great Fall. How he fell, like Ghatotkoch! Just imagine what would have happened if he had caught up with us!

"He just narrowly missed us," said Habul. "Otherwise, he would have made mincemeat of us all!"

"Made mincemeat of us all!" Teni mimicked Habul. "Not so easy. I am Teni Mukherjee of Patoldanga. Just a few jujitsu tricks and he would have become mango pulp. Or perhaps flat, like biscuits."

Kyabla started laughing.

"Kyabla, are you laughing?" Teni let out a roar.

How clever Kyabla was! He replied, "Me? That was Pyala."

"Pyala?"

Why should I laugh? My tummy was hurting after all those sweets from the yogic pot. Maybe a few ants had entered my stomach too. I made a glum face and said, "Why should I laugh?"

"Yes, remember," said Teni. "If you laugh without reason, I will take out those big teeth of yours. Issh...sh," sighed Teni, "That Gajeshwar had a narrow escape. If he had stepped into the train, he would have learnt what it means to cross the way of people from Patoldanga. If I ever meet him again..."

Who could have known that we really would meet him again? And I, Pyalaram of Patoldanga, would have been happier if we had never met.

The train reached Ramgarh after a little while.

Kyabla's uncle had told us to take a bullock-cart. But we, boys from Calcutta, on a cart! Shame, shame!

"It's only six miles," said Teni. "Come, let us walk."

"Right, right!" I said, "Let's walk in the shadow of the woods, listening to the birds singing..."

Kyabla said, "The scent of flowers, a gentle breeze..."

Teni said, "Ripe mangoes on the trees by the road..."

"And," added Habul, "the owners of the trees chasing us with big sticks."

"Ish...sh!" cried Teni, disgusted. "Just as I was getting into the right mood, thinking of all those ripe mangoes and pears, you messed it all up. Can't you think of anything better than sticks and stones? I don't know why I agreed to come with idiots like you. Now start walking."

Loaded with suitcases and bedding, we started walking. But it is one thing to walk in a park in the evening, and quite another to walk six miles with suitcases and bedding. Before we had gone half a mile, my tummy began to ache.

"Tenida, can't we rest for a while?"

"Not a bad idea," Teni replied immediately. "Besides, I feel a little hungry. We can have a little snack. What about you, Kyabla?" Teni gave a sideways glance at Kyabla's suitcase. He had already seen a tin of biscuits in it.

Kyabla held the suitcase tightly under his arm. "What do you mean, a little snack? Didn't you just eat eight *samosas* at the Ramgarh station?"

"So what?" said Teni, snatching the suitcase from under Kyabla's arm. Are you saying that I should travel six miles on eight samosas?"

He sat under a tree and opened the suitcase. Out came the tin, and a dozen crisp cream cracker biscuits. What can one do? We also sat down for a snack. Teni finished most of the biscuits, leaving only titbits for us. Only Kyabla did not have anything. He sat and sulked.

Six miles! Quite a long way! Habul had two loaves of bread with him, but those too were soon gone. But Teni was still hungry. Whenever he saw a roadside shop, he sat down and said, "Take out some money, Pyala. I am too hungry to walk!"

After about four miles, we started climbing the hills. We began to walk up a narrow road. Saal trees grew on both sides. After some time, we had a creepy feeling.

Kyabla said, "Do you know, Tenida, forests like these often have tigers in them."

Teni became a trifle pale. "Stop this nonsense," he said.

"I've heard about bears," said Habul.

"Hmm" said Teni.

"And hippopotamus too, I guess," I added.

"Shut up, Pyala," shouted Teni. "Do you think I am an ass? How can a hippopotamus live in a jungle?"

"What if there are ghosts?" I said.

"Ghost yourself," said Teni. "Why should ghosts live here, when there are no men around to scare?"

"What if the ghost likes you? You are our leader, after all. He might want to come and scare you, Tenida."

Teni immediately stretched out a long hand to grip Kyabla's ears. Kyabla dodged, Teni stepped on a heap of cowdung and–srrr...dham! I felt like clapping my hands in joy, when...out came a six-foot tall figure from the woods.

Thin like a stick, dark as coal, long hair on his head, a terrible smile on a terrible face! A ghost! A ghost must have come out of the forest just when we were talking about them!

"Oh my god!" I ran with all my might. Kyabla sprang onto a tree, Teni tried to stand up, slipped on the dung and fell once again, and Habul shut his eyes and shouted, "Bhoot! Bhoot! Ram, Ram, Ram!"

"Ha-ha-ha" laughed the figure. "Why are you getting scared? I am Jhanturam of Jhanto Hills. Babu had sent me a letter, so I came to receive you all."

By then, I was half-a-mile away and Kyabla was on the topmost branch of the tree. Habul went on chanting 'Ram, Ram,' while Teni lay, motionless, on the cowdung. He must have fainted.

The figure spoke once again. "Don't be scared, babu. I am Jhanturam of Jhanto Hills, your servant."

shoes that walked

What an awful mess! That rascal Jhanturam was not a ghost, yet he scared us no end! I kept trembling for half an hour.

Teni stood up, cowdung all over him. Kyabla, bitten by ants, came down from the tree scratching his legs. Habul's knees were knocking into each other.

And, since I had run several miles, my liver wanted to jump out of my body.

The first to recover was Teni. "Jhanturam?" he cried, "Then why do you look like a ghost?"

"What can I do, Babu? God has made me like this."

"God?" mimicked Teni. "God's handiwork can never be so bad. You were made by demons. Understand?"

Jhanturam did not object to that.

Kyabla said, "But what were you doing in that bush?"

Jhanturam grinned, showing his uneven teeth and said, "I was going to the station, but on my way I felt too sleepy to go on. I was sleeping by the side of the road, till some mosquitoes went up my nose. I woke up and saw you coming. So I came towards you, but you got such a fright..." and he started laughing his nasty laugh.

"Okay, that's enough," said Kyabla. "What teeth you have–like a row of radishes. Now show us the way to Jhanto Hills."

Really, Jhanto Hills is a wonderful place. The name may be awful, but how can one not be overwhelmed by its beauty? On three sides, the *palash* trees on the hills were ablaze with red palash flowers, as if the hills were all aflame! Birds were flying around, and what beautiful colours they had! The lake in front of the bungalow was full of cool, blue water, where water plants nodded their heads. On the other side, their heads held high and poised like snakes, *pankaudis* were diving into the water.

The bungalow was on a small hillock, with trees on three sides. It had red brick walls, green doors and windows, a roof of red tiles. It looked like another head of red palash flowers, with a few green leaves peeping out. Such a beautiful place, such sweet breeze, such a picturesque house–how could this place be haunted? It's just not possible.

The rooms were also nicely decorated. Tables, chairs, deckchairs, dressing tables, and a thick carpet too! Jhanturam made up four beds neatly in two of the rooms. We sat and relaxed on the cane chairs in the verandah. Jhanturam brought us omelettes and tea. "Will you have fish or chicken for lunch?" he asked.

"Chicken! Chicken!" we cried in a chorus.

Teni's mouth was watering. "Ush...sh," he said, sucking his tongue. "Listen, make it quick, understand? It is twelve now, my tummy is rumbling angrily. If you make me wait too long, I might start eating the tables and chairs."

"Oh yes, you can easily do that!" said Habul.

"What? What did you say, Habul?"

"Nothing, nothing," said Habul. "I was only saying, Jhantu can cook very fast."

Jhanturam left the room. Teni said, "Well, he looks terrible, but the man seems to be good."

"Oh yes," I said, "He is taking good care of us. If he serves chicken everyday, we'll put on weight in a week."

"Don't you try putting on weight, Pyala," said Teni. "You suffer from flu every month, taking *Kabiraji* medicines all the time. Rich food won't suit you. From tomorrow, it will be only vegetable stew for you. What if you suddenly fall sick? You'll land us in trouble in this place—miles away from anywhere."

33

"No need to lose sleep over my health," I replied with a glum face. "If I die, I'll die eating chicken."

"And you'll be born again as a chicken," joked Kyabla. "Cock-a-doodle-doo!"

What a stupid joke! I sat there, furious, scratching my nose, while the others laughed at me.

It was two in the afternoon when we sat down for lunch. Jhantu was an excellent cook. As soon as we ate, our eyes grew heavy with sleep. We lay down on the soft beds and dropped off.

When Jhantu woke us up and handed us steaming cups of tea, the sun had set behind the hills. The forests of saal and palash were dark, and the water of the lake had turned the colour of lead. This beautiful place which fascinated us when we arrived now had a sullen, scary look. Crickets were singing in the bushes and in the forest behind the bungalow.

We had planned to walk by the lake in the evening, but now all of us felt uneasy. We thought of Calcutta, with lights shining in every street, and in every house. There, crowds would be gathering before the cinema halls. Here, darkness was gathering all around us, the crickets were singing louder and louder, and an inexpressible terror had spread on all sides.

Sitting in the verandah, we tried to talk to each other, but could not really work ourselves into a cheerful mood.

Jhanturam lit a lantern and placed it in front of us. But it only made the darkness appear denser.

At last, Teni said, "Come, let's sing a song."

"Not a bad idea," said Kyabla. "Lets sing together, in a chorus." And he started singing

"*Saare jahanse acchha, Hindustan hamara...*"

At once the three of us joined in. What a racket! No one could call our voices melodious—least of all Teni's. A story goes that once Teni had started singing a *kirtan*, but before he had finished even the first part of the song, the pet *koel*, which his neighbours kept in a cage, died of a heart attack. Now our racket made Jhanturam come running, scared out of his wits.

I suppose we were all thinking the same thing. Even if the bungalow on Jhanto Hills was haunted, the ghosts would not stay here for long if they had to put up with such 'music'.

But that night: Kyabla and I were in one room, Habul and Teni in the other. A dim lantern stood in our room and, in its yellow light, the chairs, tables and the dressing table looked strange. I felt choked with fear. I turned this way and that. I could hear Teni's snores—his nose was practising the scales. Through the glass window, I saw the stars shining brightly atop the dark hills. I don't know when I fell asleep.

Suddenly I heard a sound. Tap, tap, tap.

I woke up with a start. Someone was walking around.

Where?

Here, in this room. Someone wearing boots was walking around this room.

I turned up the lantern. No, no one could be seen. But I could still hear the sound of the boots. Yes, someone was surely walking around.

I shouted, "Kyabla!"

Kyabla jumped up. "What? What is it?"

"Someone is walking in the room!"

What a daring young boy that Kyabla was! He jumped out of the bed and at once a mouse ran out through a hole in the door.

Kyabla laughed. "What a coward you are, Pyala! That mouse was moving inside an old pair of torn shoes. You got so scared by that sound?"

"Of course not!" I said boldly. "You thought I was scared? Forget the mice, even if the *brahmarakshas* comes..."

I couldn't finish my words. Exactly at that moment, we heard an inhuman cry of pain. And it was followed by an immense roar of laughter. No one has ever heard laughter like that. It seemed as if it arose from the depths of the earth, and the entire bungalow on Jhanto Hills shook with the sound.

The Night of Terror

W hen the terrible laughter stopped, we felt as if the bungalow was still shaking. I had dived under the sheets, quick as lightning. Even brave Kyabla had jumped into his bed. My hands and feet had turned cold, my teeth were chattering. Kyabla, too, did not look too well.

It was a full ten minutes before we could speak. Kyabla was the first to recover his nerves. In a dry voice, he said, "What's up, Pyala?"

"Ghos...ghost!" I said from beneath the sheets.

Kyabla said, "But why should ghosts come and laugh here, without rhyme or reason?"

"This is a haunted bungalow," I said. "Why should they laugh elsewhere? Besides, even ghosts need a place to laugh."

Kyabla scratched his head. "But does that mean they can laugh like that in the middle of the night and wake up people?"

"Of course, ghosts always laugh at midnight," I said. "Do you expect them to sit in College Square in the afternoon and laugh?"

"That's what they should do," said Kyabla. "Then we can meet them and settle the matter once and for all. But no, they must start laughing at a most ungodly hour! And what a laugh–haa haa, ho ho, hou hou. Pyala, why do you think ghosts laugh like that at an ungodly hour?"

I lost my temper. "How do I know? Why don't you go and ask the ghost?"

Kyabla jumped down from the bed. "Let's do that. Let's go and look for the ghost at once. We'll also tell him that four gentlemen are now staying in the bungalow, and that it's heartless to spoil their sleep at night."

My hair stood on end. "What are you saying Kyabla? Have you lost your mind?"

"Of course not!" said Kyabla. I had to admit that he had a lot of guts. He smiled a little and said, "You know, Pyala, I think ghosts are also scared of men."

"What rubbish!"

"No, it's true. Why else do ghosts avoid big cities like Calcutta? Why don't they ever show even a hair of their ghostly beards during the day? Why do they sit outside our rooms and laugh? Why don't they dare to come inside?"

I felt choked with fright. "Ram, Ram, don't even utter such words, Kyabla. Haven't you heard that laugh? Don't invite them. What if two severed heads appear in the room and start dancing?"

Kyabla, that dangerous boy, said without hesitation, "Let them dance. I have never seen the dance of severed heads. I'll surely enjoy it. Okay, I am counting upto three. If the ghosts have enough courage, let them come inside and start dancing! I challenge them. One, two..."

What was Kyabla doing! Making fun of ghosts, who can read minds! Stiff with fear, I hid my face in the sheets. They'd come, right now...

"Three," said Kyabla.

I had turned to marble beneath the sheets. Something horrible was going to happen. They would come, surely!

Nothing happened. Perhaps the ghosts did not pay any attention to a small fellow like Kyabla.

Kyabla said, "See? I challenged them, but they did not dare to come. Come with me. Teni and Habul must be up by now. Let us go, all four of us, and meet those ghosts."

I felt choked with fear again. "Kyabla, you're surely going to die."

Kyabla did not listen to me. He pulled me up by my hand. "Get up," he said.

I held on to the bed for dear life. "Are you crazy, Kyabla? Go, lie down."

But Kyabla would not listen. He came over to my bed and started pulling me. "Do you think we will sit quietly and let those ghosts wake us up at midnight?"

He pulled so hard that I landed on the floor, sheets, pillow and all. "What are you doing?" I shouted.

Kyabla pulled me up on my feet. "Let's go and see what Teni and Habul are doing in the next room." He picked up the lantern and started walking.

What could I do? I prayed to all the gods I knew and followed Kyabla. If I were to stay alone in the dark room, I'd have surely fainted, or even died right away.

The door of the next room was ajar. Kyabla went inside and cried out, "Hey, where have they gone?"

There was no one in the room! Both the beds were empty. But all the doors and windows were closed, save the door connecting the two rooms. They couldn't have gone anywhere without passing our room.

"Where do you think they have gone?" asked Kyabla.

I was trembling. "Surely the ghosts have made them vanish," I said. "Maybe they have wrung Habul and Teni's necks and sucked their blood by now!"

Even Kyabla looked uneasy. He looked around and said, "This is puzzling. Surely two solid, living men cannot vanish into thin air?"

Right at that moment...

Kaank! Kaank! What a strange noise. As if a snake had caught a frog right inside the room. Kyabla jumped, and the lantern nearly fell from his hands. I jumped onto Teni's bed.

Again that noise, Kaank! Kaank!

This had to be the ghost! My spleen was shaking, as if I had malaria. I shut my eyes tightly, expecting something ghastly to happen. But Kyabla started laughing.

Startled, I opened my eyes. Kyabla was peering under Habul's bed, lantern in hand.

"Look Pyala," he said, still laughing, "Our leader Teni is hiding under the bed. The two are holding on to each other, scared of ghosts."

Teni and Habul came out, their faces streaked with dust and cobwebs.

"Bravo Tenida," said Kyabla. "Aren't you our leader, the hero of Patoldanga?"

Teni had collected himself by then. Dusting himself, he said, "Okay, that's enough. We went under the bed because we had a plan."

A cockroach was walking on Habul's shoulder. He flicked it away and said, "Yes, yes, we had a plan."

"Okay then, tell us about it," said Kyabla. "*Mutlab batlao*," he repeated in Hindi. Kyabla had lived in the Hindi belt for quite sometime, and he had this habit of lapsing into Hindi, now and then.

Teni had settled himself on the bed. Confidently, he said, "Can't you see? We were watching from under the bed. If a ghost had entered the room..."

"We would have caught hold of his feet," said Habul, "and given such a pull that he would have fallen ..."

"Flat," finished Teni.

"Heh heh heh," Kyabla started laughing.

Teni got angry. "Stop laughing like that, Kyabla. How dare you insult me? Take care, I say, or will send your nose to..."

Teni probably wanted to send Kyabla's nose to Nashik, when a horrible thing happened. We heard the sound of glass breaking. Shards from the broken window pane scattered on the floor and a white, ball-like thing landed inside. It rolled towards Kyabla and stopped near his feet.

In the dim light from the lantern, I could see what it was. A human skull.

I screamed and hit the floor at once. Habul and Teni disappeared under the bed once again. Only Kyabla stood there with the lantern in his hand.

Immediately, that terrible roar of laughter rose again. And the bungalow on Jhanto Hills began to shake with the sound.

Who are you, Laughing Man?

I need not describe how we spent the rest of the night.

I don't know what happened to Teni and Habul, I had fainted right away. While I was lying there, I felt as if two men, as tall as palm trees, were carrying me off. One of them was saying, "We will make a curry out of this one." The other said, "Phooh! This one is like a stick, he hardly has any flesh. We can use him like a herb for seasoning."

I think I was crying my eyes out. Suddenly I jumped up. Someone was splashing water on my face. How icy the water was! If any one splashed such water on a tiger's face, the tiger would surely drop down, senseless.

But my senses had to return. They were forced to return. Who else but Kyabla could do such a thing? He had come with a can from the garden and sprinkled me all over with ice-cold water.

"Stop, stop, will you?"

Kyabla sprinkled some more water on my face and asked, "Have you cooled off?"

"What do you mean, cooled off! My whole body is freezing!" I had to jump out of the way of the watering can.

I could see the light of dawn through the glass windows. Our nightmare was finally over! The water in the lake was blue, the sky above it reddish in the early morning light. Birds were singing sweetly all around us, the saal and palash trees, fresh with dew, looked like a picture.

Drying myself, I thought, "Why should such a beautiful place house such terrible ghosts?"

Even while I was thinking such thoughts, Kyabla's can was doing its duty. Hearing a commotion, I looked around and saw Teni and Habul emerging from under the bed, drenched.

Kyabla laughed. "Isn't this the perfect way to bring you back to your senses?"

"Shut up, Kyabla," thundered Teni. "Who told you we had fainted? We were discussing our plans in peace, and you spoilt it all." Teni sneezed. "Ooof," he groaned. "I hope I don't get double pneumonia."

We asked Jhanturam about the ghost business, but he was of no help. He did not stay in the bungalow in the night. His house was about a mile away. He had left after dinner, and returned in the morning.

"No use asking him anything. He is an idiot," said Teni.

"Who knows, maybe he is a ghost himself," added Habul. "Can't you see how he looks? As if he has just climbed down a palm tree."

I jumped. "Really? Can he really be a ghost?"

"Fools, both of you," said Teni. "Don't you know ghosts always run at the sight of fire? Jhantu lighted the stove and made tea. In the evening, you ate the rice and chicken he made. Have you forgotten?"

We hardly ate any chicken, since Teni had eaten most of it. We only got a few bones. But what was the use of complaining?

"I don't care whether Jhanturam is a ghost or not," I spoke up. "All I want to say is, if I must die, I will die in Patoldanga. I am not ready to die here, at the hands of ghosts. I am returning to Calcutta today."

Habul also got excited. "Yes, yes. Me too."

Teni scratched his long, hooked nose.

"You stay on if you want," I said. "Let the ghosts make *handi kebab* out of you, or cutlets, or roasts, I don't mind. I am leaving today."

"Well," said Teni. "But this place is so beautiful, the food so delicious. These ghosts have spoiled everything."

"Why do the ghosts love to stay in these forests?" said Habul. "Why don't they come to Calcutta? They would have enjoyed themselves, and so would we. Just imagine what might happen if they cast a spell on our teachers? We would not have to do any homework."

"Right you are. But who can make the ghosts understand this?"

"Okay, let us return," sighed Teni. "But I am feeling very sorry. Such a nice place, such nice meals. Have you seen how much butter Jhantu puts on the toasts? We would have put on some weight if we stayed on."

"The ghosts will put on weight before we do," I said.

Teni lifted the plate before him and scraped off the butter under it. Licking his fingers, he let out a heartbreaking sigh. "Today is final, then?"

"Yes, today," said Habul and I, together.

But we had forgotten all about Kyabla. Where was he? There was no sign of him since he gone in the morning after waking us up with the water can.

"Where is Kyabla?" I asked.

Teni started. "Oh yes, where is he? I haven't seen him since morning!"

"He was making fun of ghosts," said Habul. "I hope the ghosts haven't spirited him away?"

"Ghosts are not fools," said Teni, wrinkling up his nose. "No ghost will be able to stand Kyabla. But where is he? Has he already run away, leaving us?"

Just then, we heard loud singing:

On the roof dances the crow,

And the crane dances with him,

Ho Rama! Ho Ho Rama!

What a song! I nearly fell off the chair. Have the ghosts come to attack us in broad daylight?

Not ghosts—it was Kyabla! He had arrived from somewhere, a big grin on his face.

"Where have you been?" asked Teni. "And why are you bellowing like a bull?"

"Wait," said Kyabla, and looked at the cups and dishes before us with sorry eyes. "You've already finished breakfast? Nothing left for me?"

"Ask Jhanturam," said Teni. "But first tell us, where have you been?"

Kyabla smiled a mischievous smile and said, "I went looking for ghosts. No sign of them, but I found a packet of peanuts. Half of the pack is only shells, the rest are nuts. Which means they could finish only half of it."

"Who?" I asked like an idiot.

"The same people who had thrown the skull from the bushes outside. If they are ghosts, I must admit they are quite modern ghosts, Tenida. They eat nuts, popcorn, chops, too."

Teni said, "That means..."

"That means all this is the work of some mischief-maker," said Kyabla. "He must have laughed that horrible laugh, thrown the skull into the room. He badly wants us to leave this place. You are our leader, the champion of Patoldanga, will you be scared by such people and run away?"

"Are you sure they are not ghosts?"

"Absolutely," said Kyabla. "Who has ever heard of ghosts eating chops and nuts? And smoking *beedis* too. I found some beedi butts.

"Then they are men, not ghosts," said Teni. He jumped up and stood very straight, sticking out his chest. "And we will teach them a lesson or two. Come with me, quick march!"

He gave my hand such a tug that I fell on the floor. Habul made a face like an owl and said, "Where do we have to go?"

"We must meet them. We are Calcutta boys, how dare they scare us like this? Let's go and look around."

Kyabla said, "But my breakfast?"

"You'll have it along with lunch. Now come on!"

Habul and Kyabla stood up. Then a strange thing happened in broad daylight. A voice came floating from above our heads, a rough voice saying, "Well, well, well." It was followed by a mocking laugh. "Ha! ha! ha!"

Who spoke? Who laughed? We could not see a single soul. Who could it be?

on the ROOf Dances the cRow

It was not yet light, and yet, not dark. It was eight in the morning, and the sun was slowly lighting up all sides. We looked at the roof, but there was not even a sparrow there. Yet the sound had come through the roof.

How was it possible?

Were we mad? Or did Jhanturam put something in the tea? But Kyabla did not have tea with us, yet he too had heard the sound.

For four minutes, the four of us sat like four tops. We were not spinning, but whatever grey matter there was inside our heads was going round and round. I was happy enough in Patoldanga, having fish with patol. Why did I listen to Teni and land up here? These ghosts would surely be the end of me!

After three more minutes, I turned to Kyabla and asked, "What now?"

Habul glanced up at once and said, "Yes, now speak up."

Teni's hooked nose hung forward, like a parrot's beak. He moistened his lips with his tongue and said, "Well, you see, if I encounter a man, I can send him flying with one blow. But if it's a ghost then, er, how can one fight ghosts?"

"Besides, ghosts do not follow boxing rules," I added.

"Will you shut up, tuna fish?" scolded Teni.

I get furious when someone calls me tuna fish. If I were not weak with the fear of ghosts, I would have surely called Teni a carp.

But Kyabla was not one to accept defeat.

He ran to the lawn in front of the bungalow. Craning his neck, he looked upwards for some time. "Got it!" he cried. He sounded very pleased. "Remember what I sang? *On the roof dances the crow, and the crane dances with him?*"

"What do you mean?" asked Teni.

"Oh, it's as clear as water. Someone was sitting on the roof. He must have laughed that horrible laugh."

"Then where did he disappear?"

"Why don't you come down? I'll show you. Or are you too scared? Say 'Ram Ram' then."

"Scared? Who's scared?" said Teni, not looking too happy. "It's just that my legs have pins and needles."

"Oh yes, lots of people get pins and needles when they hear about ghosts," laughed Kyabla.

After that, what could the leader do? Teni made a face like a fried egg and went to the lawn. Habul and I followed him.

"Can you see that *peepul* tree behind the bungalow? Now look at that thick branch. See how it comes right over the bungalow's roof. Someone climbed that branch and landed on the bungalow roof. He must have listened to our conversation. Then he laughed that horrible laugh and went back the same way."

Habul nodded. "I think you're right. Can't you see the fresh green leaves lying on the roof? Someone must have climbed that branch."

"Okay, but where did he go?" asked Teni.

"I am sure they have a place somewhere near. We must go and ferret it out. Are you ready?"

Teni scratched his nose and said, "Well, I was saying..."

"What you are saying, Tenida, is that you don't have the guts," said Kyabla, smiling. "Okay, I will go alone."

Teni laughed a dry laugh. "Shut up, Kyabla, don't talk nonsense," he said. "I was saying that if only we had a few rifles or revolvers..."

I was about to say, what use would guns be before ghosts? Besides, Teni handling a gun would mean the end of the three of us. He would surely shoot us down before he killed any ghosts.

Kyabla spoke before me, "Why do you need a gun, Tenida? Haven't you knocked down huge sahibs in fights? What use is a gun to you?"

At other times, Teni would have been happy to hear this. Now his fried-egg face started looking like aalu chaat. In a resigned whisper, he said, "Okay, let's go."

"Don't worry, Tenida," said Kyabla. "I am sure these are bad men trying to scare us. Shouldn't we, the four heroes from Patoldanga, teach them a lesson before we return to Calcutta?"

Habul gave a big sigh. "Who knows who will teach a lesson to whom!"

But Kyabla had already started walking. Teni, with a face like a martyr, walked behind him. Habul too followed them. I, Pyalaram, who suffers from malaria, had no wish to be involved in such dare-devil acts. But how could I stay alone in the bungalow? If I heard that horrible, ear-splitting laughter once more, I would surely have a heart attack. If Jhanturam was there, I might have stayed back. But he had gone to the nearby village to buy chicken. I would be the last person to sit alone and fall in the clutches of ghosts.

But where would we find the den of the mischief-makers?

The three of us walked on. There was a large forest behind the bungalow, stretching for miles. The trees were not too high and came upto our heads. The trees were mostly saal and palash, and in some places, there were bushes of wild flowers. A narrow, dirt road ran in the middle of the forest. Who knew who took this road? Who knew whether their feet touched the ground, or not?

My heart started beating furiously. I felt as if I could see a ghost coming out of any of the bushes. But nothing happened. As I listened to the birds and saw soft, sweet sunlight filter through the trees, I felt the fear leave me.

At first, I was quite careful, walking by Kyabla's side. Then suddenly I saw a *boinchi* tree, full of boinchis so ripe that they had turned black. I tore one and tasted it. It tasted wonderful! I ate another one, then another...

I had finished about fifty of them when I discovered that my friends had gone ahead. I hurried to catch up with them when I saw, peeping from a bush near me...

What was that, long and white! Must be a tail. A squirrel's tail.

I love squirrels. My friend Volta had one. It used to ride on his shoulders and sleep in his pockets. They make very nice pets. I had always wanted a squirrel!

I walked slowly, looking the other way. Then, phut! I caught hold of the tail and gave a mighty pull!

But where was the squirrel? The moment I pulled, there was a deafening shout of pain. The next moment, I had received a hundred megaton slap on my cheek!

The world danced before my eyes. I saw fields of yellow mustard flowers, and flowers of all other kinds, till...

I fell down in a dead faint. Right there, in the bush. Who knows, I might have died!

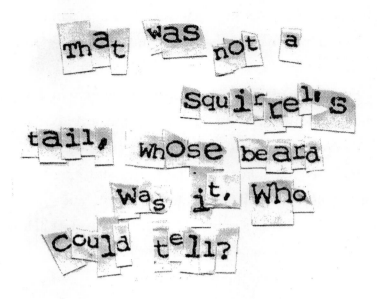

That was not a squirrel's tail, whose beard was it, who could tell?

When I came to, I found I was lying on a bed in the bungalow. By my head stood Jhantu, fanning me. Kyabla was sitting near my feet, looking at me with narrowed eyes, while Teni sat, watching me closely, on a chair by the side of the bed.

"Ouch!" I cried. Jhantu's fan had hit me right on the nose.

Teni jumped from his chair. "So you are not dead yet? Thank God!"

"Die? Why should he die?" Kyabla chipped in. "He just fainted for a while. Didn't I ask you, Tenida, to hold a burning chilli in front of his nose? He would have been fit in a jiffy!"

"Don't talk of chillies, said Teni. "The way he lay there, his teeth sticking out! I thought it was the end of our Pyala from Patoldanga."

"Heh heh heh!" laughed that idiot Jhantu, making a horrible noise. "Dadababu fainted in fright!"

"Enough!" cried Kyabla. "Don't you too start acting smart. Now go, bring a cup of hot milk. Quick!"

Jhantu put down the fan and went out.

There was still a mist before my eyes and a terrible pain in my right jaw. God, what a slap! I wouldn't be surprised if I found two of my teeth wobbling. What was our maths teacher's smack compared to a slap like this? A pinch of scented snuff!

To think that I, Pyalaram of Patoldanga, who is down with fever every other day and can have nothing but vegetable stew, had survived such a demonic slap!

"Well then, tuna fish," said Tenida, "tell us why you let out such a shout and fainted."

In spite of the pain, I was really angry. How dare anyone call me a tuna fish?

"Okay, fine. So what if I am a tuna?" I said. "If you re-

ceived such a terrific slap, you would have become a
pomfret."

Kyabla was stunned. "But who slapped you, Pyala?"

"A ghost."

"A ghost!" laughed Teni. "Does the ghost not have better
things to do? Why should he come and slap you, and that
too in broad daylight? What's wrong with you Pyala, your
head or your tummy?"

"Must be his tummy," said Kyabla. " Just look at him,
thin as a twig. But since we came here, he has been stuffing
himself with chicken and eggs. Little wonder his head reeled
and he fell down. And now he is making up ghost stories."

"Right you are," agreed Teni.

I held my right jaw and sat up. "So you don't believe
me?"

"Of course not," replied Teni. "As if the ghost couldn't
find a better cheek to slap!"

Kyabla nodded his head. "Absolutely! Why should the
ghost choose you instead of Tenida, our leader? Isn't that
insulting the leader?"

Teni glared at Kyabla. "Are you joking?"

Kyabla leapt away until at least five feet of floor was
between them.

"Joking? With you? Don't I care for my own poor cheek?
All I said was, whatever the ghost wants to do–shake hands

or start boxing–he should follow etiquette and do it with the leader."

Teni did not look too pleased. He made a face like a dish of *upma* and said, "Okay, okay, that's enough. But you Pyala, no eggs for you from today, I tell you. Just plain vegetable stew for lunch, and barley water for dinner. Today you fainted, what if you die tomorrow!"

"To hell with your stew and barley!" I fumed. " Why don't you believe me? I tell you it was a ghost who slapped me."

"He did, did he?" said Kyabla.

"Now stop spinning yarns," said Teni.

"Am I making this up?" I said. "Why is my right cheek burning then?"

"So what?" said Teni. "Our tooth aches, head reels, ears sing. Does that mean ghosts are beating us up all the time?"

Now I was really hurt. It was bad enough to be hit by a ghost, but what could be worse than your own friends laughing at you? Or were they were envying me because the ghost had simply ignored them?

"But why don't you listen to me?" I was now quite agitated. "Let me tell you what happened. You people went ahead, while I fell back, munching fruits. Suddenly I saw the tail of a squirrel in a bush. Phut! I caught hold of the tail..."

"Wham! The squirrel smacked you," Teni roared with

laughter. Kyabla, too, started rocking to and fro, making a sound like jackals quarrelling.

What an insult! My insides started dancing within me. And just at that moment, I caught sight of the thing in my right hand. In my fist was...

A clump of whitish hair! I must have torn off a bit of the squirrel's tail. I held out my hand, "Look at this. See what I am holding in my hand!"

Kyabla leapt forward. Teni stretched out his paw and snatched away the clump of hair. And then he cried out, "But this, this is..."

Kyabla shouted even louder, "Someone's beard!"

"Grey beard," said Teni.

"With a brownish tinge," added Kyabla. "A smoker's beard."

"Ghost's beard," whispered Teni.

Ghost's beard! I could feel my hands and feet going cold. What have I done? I had taken a ghost's beard to be a squirrel's tail and torn it off! No wonder he had given me such a terrific slap!

But would I get away with only a swollen cheek? Surely this was a much-cared-for beard. Perhaps the ghost sat on a tree in dark nights, patting his beard and singing *Khambaj ragini*. Not that I knew what Khambaj ragini was like. But doesn't a name like Khambaj somehow suggest that it would be a favourite of ghosts? And now I had torn off his beloved beard. What if he came at midnight and tore off my hair? I hit the bed once again.

But Kyabla was looking at the hair keenly. "Tenida, do ghosts smoke?"

"Why not? Why shouldn't they?" asked Teni.

"No, I mean...," Kyabla scratched his head. "Don't they say that ghosts cannot touch fire? How then could the ghost smoke? Besides, I have a feeling that I have seen a beard like this somewhere, white, with a brownish tinge..."

Kyabla was going to say something more, but suddenly Jhantu entered with a pair of shoes. He held them up right before Teni's face and said, "Look, Dadababu!"

"Look at this fool!" Teni cried out. "We told you to bring a cup of hot milk for Pyala, and you thrust a pair of shoes under my nose. Am I supposed to chew them or what?"

"Ram Ram!" said Jhantu. "Dogs chew up shoes, why should you? I only want to know where has Habulbabu gone? His shoes were outside but I couldn't see him any- where. Then I saw a letter inside the shoes, so I've brought them to you."

I suddenly remembered that I had not seen Habul Sen since I woke up. But why a letter inside shoes?

Kyabla said, "Here, I can see something like a note

inside the shoe. What's the matter, Tenida? Where has Habul gone?"

"Wait, wait," said Teni, pulling out the folded paper. "Let me read the note."

But as soon as his eyes ran through the note, they jumped right up to the middle of his forehead. Teni gulped thrice and wailed, "Kyabla, we're finished."

"Finished? What do you mean?"

"Habul is gone."

"Gone where?" Kyabla and I cried together. "What is in the letter Tenida? What does it say?"

Teni's voice quivered. "Listen to this." He read out:

'We have vanished Habul Sen. If you pack up your bags immediately and leave for Calcutta today, you will get him back, unharmed, before you leave. Otherwise we will vanish all four of you, forever. We are warning all of you before-hand, don't blame us later.

From Ghachang Fu, ferocious Chinese Bandit.'

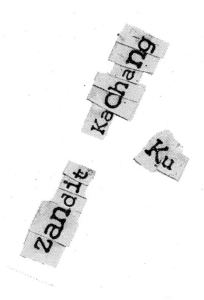

Teni sat down on the floor. A bee droned round his big nose for sometime, perhaps considering it as a site for its hive. Suddenly such a frightful sound came out of his nose that the bee took fright and fled.

Our leader was in a sorry state. "My god," he wailed, "we have fallen into the hands of a Chinese bandit! Ghosts would have been better."

My hands and feet were about to sink into my tummy. I piped in, "And look at his name: Ghachang Fu. 'Ghachang'– that's how he will chop off our heads and 'Fu'–blow them away".

Jhantu was looking at us. He asked, "What is the matter, Babu?"

"The matter is serious," replied Kyabla. "Jhantu, do you know if there are any bandits here?"

"Bandits? Dacoits?" said Jhantu. "Why should dacoits come here? This place doesn't have dacoits."

"No, it doesn't," mimicked Teni, making a face like *kofta* curry. "Then from where did Ghachang Fu appear?"

Kyabla said, "All that is bluff, Tenida. Why should a Chinese Bandit come to a bungalow in Hazaribag? The idea seems straight out of a Bengali detective novel."

How smart Kyabla was! Nothing could unsettle him.

"Bengali novel?" said Teni, scratching his jaw. "That means...?"

"That means those people must be reading endless mystery stories, the kind where the detective drives a submarine in a village pond. One of my uncles is a police officer at Lal Bazar. Once I asked him, 'Where do these detectives live?' He got furious and said they live inside the head of people who smoke you-know-what!"

"But what have detectives got to do with Ghachang Fu?" said Teni.

"Oh, everything," said Kyabla. "Those who have written this letter read those detective stories. That's why they have played this trick on us."

"But why? Why are they trying to make us leave this place? And where have they taken Habul?"

"That's the mystery, and we must solve it," said Kyabla. "Those mischief-mongers must be near us. And they have done us a favour by sending this letter, Tenida."

"Favour? What favour?"

"It is now clear that there are no ghosts in this bungalow. None at all. Only some rascals, who are hiding nearby, need the bungalow for some purpose. Our arrival has disturbed their activities, that's why they are trying to force us to leave. But..." and here Kyabla paused and took a deep breath, "should we leave because of some rascals, Tenida? Never. We will make them understand that if they are Ghachang Fu, then we are Kachang Ku."

"Kachang Ku?" I said, "What's that?"

"Chinese bandits more ferocious than Ghachang Fu."

I made a glum face. "When did we turn Chinese? And why on earth should we become bandits?"

"Okay then, if they are bandits then we are Zandits."

"Zandits?" said Teni, trying to drive away the bee which had come back and was flying round his nose once again. "What is a Zandit?"

"Those who take in bandits like snuff and sneeze them out are called Zandits."

Teni stood up. "Look here Kyabla, stop joking. If they really are robbers..."

"If they were dacoits, they would have shown their

strength by now. Do you think they would sit in bushes eating peanuts, or throw in skulls wrapped in paper? They are absolute cowards."

"Then how could they vanish Habul Sen?"

"They must have played a trick. It won't take us long to discover what that is. Tenida..."

"What?"

"No more delay. Let's go. Ready?"

"Ready for what?" asked Teni.

"We must Kachang Ku that Ghachang Fu. Right now."

Teni wasn't feeling too bold. He mumbled, "How can we do that?"

"Oh, we will find a way. Their den must be close to the bungalow. We must invade that den."

"What if they shoot at us?"

"We will throw stones at them," said Kyabla, making a face. "Look, it is not so easy to get hold of pistols in real life as it is in detective stories. But yes, we might take a few sticks. Jhantu, do we have sticks in the bungalow?"

Jhantu had been listening to us all long. "Yes," he said, "And some spears too."

"Then bring them, quick!"

"What will you do with sticks and spears, babu?" asked a surprised Jhantu.

"We will kill foxes."

"Why? Do you eat fox meat?"

"Don't ask so many questions," said Kyabla, sounding angry. "Do what I said. Bring those sticks."

Jhantu went inside. Teni said in a dry voice, "Kyabla, I don't like this. If we fall into any danger..."

"Oh, you people are getting scared," said Kyabla, wrinkling up his nose. "Very well then, you stay in the bungalow. I am going with Pyala. See, even Pyala has more courage than you do!"

My chest swelled up, but my tummy started rumbling. Do I have to go? Okay, I will. A man dies only once. If I die, my mother and aunts will cry. The Secondary Board will also cry. Who else will give them exam fees year after year? But never mind, what are such minor losses in the face of a heroic death?

Teni heaved a deep sigh and said, "Okay then, let's go. But that beard in Pyala's hand..."

"Tobacco-stained beard," I reminded them.

"Right!" said Kyabla. "I had forgotten all about it. See, that beard itself proves that they are not Chinese. Have you ever seen a Chinaman with a beard?"

He was right! None of us has ever seen a bearded Chinaman.

Jhantu had brought two sticks and a spear. Teni took a stick and Kyabla the other. Jhantu took the spear himself.

What could I take? A piece of firewood was lying nearby. I picked that up. I would strike at least one blow before I died.

And so the team of Kachang Ku went out in search of Ghachang Fu. Again to that narrow road in the forest. We started searching the bushes to see if the owner of the beard was hiding anywhere.

But once again, my greed got the better of me. Not boinchi this time, but *kamranga* fruits.

I fell behind, as usual. We had come behind the bungalow when I caught sight of the kamranga tree. Aha! It was laden with ripe fruits!

Nearly a litre of water gushed to my mouth. A chronic malaria patient, I simply love tangy, sour fruits. I forgot all about Ghachang Fu and crept towards the tree. You can't blame me. I never get to eat kamranga in Calcutta!

The moment I stepped under the tree...Eeeek! I stepped on a huge pile of cowdung, slipped and fell flat. But what was happening? I did not land on solid ground. I kept falling...falling...

I landed on someone's neck. What a large neck it was! "Ooow!" cried the owner of the neck, and threw me down on the floor. I fainted once again.

In Gajeshwar's Grip

Fainting is not too bad, as long as red ants don't bite you. But if a whole army of them start biting, even a dead man will jump up.

I too jumped up.

At first, all I could see was darkness. I could see nothing clearly. Again, a red ant started biting my left ear. "Ooh Baba," I said, removing the ant from my ear.

At once, someone started laughing, making a sound like a croaking frog. Then the voice, which now sounded like a horse's neigh, said, "Only a red ant, and you are calling your father. Who will you call if you get bitten by a wasp? Your grandfather?"

Who was that?

A huge man was sitting some distance away from me. He laughed once again, making the same croaking sound.

"Where am I?" I asked.

"Where am I?" mimicked the man, making an ugly face and baring all his big teeth. Then he scowled like an angry owl and said, "So you are an innocent baby, are you? You landed like a brick on my back, and now you're asking where you are. Nice joke, I must say."

Now everything came back to me. The kamranga tree, slipping into the heap of dung, and then ...

All at once, I started howling. "Bow-wow-wow," I cried, "am I in the den of Bandit Ghachang Fu?"

"Ghachang Fu? What's that?" asked the man, but controlled himself immediately. "Oh yes, Babaji had written something like that in the letter."

"Babaji? Who is he?"

"Oh, you'll learn that soon enough!" The man bared his teeth once again. "Why didn't you listen to us when we told you to leave? I spent the whole night in the bushes, and mosquitoes made a feast of me. My throat is still hurting from those demonic laughs, but still you wouldn't leave. Now you will learn your lesson. I have already got hold of one of you, now you too have fallen into the trap. Now I will make *sheekh kebab* out of you."

"Sheekh kebab?"

"Or may be aalu chaat, if I want," he said, "or fowl cutlet perhaps. Or even a chop," he scratched his head thoughtfully. "But you look so unappetizing. I wonder if you will make any good dish at all."

I saw a bit of hope there. Let me make one last attempt to save my skin!

"Right you are. Don't eat me. You'll surely get indigestion. You may get cholera, you'll get rashes, diphtheria, and I won't be surprised if you get influenza too."

"Shut up," said the man. "Right now I'll take you to the cold storage, where we've kept your friend, Habul Sen. You'll stay there for some time now. Let Babaji return, and let me get hold of your two other friends. Then we will decide whether we will make *mughlai paratha* or egg upma out of you."

"Please, please don't eat me up," I pleaded. "I am not tasty at all, I tell you. I suffer from malaria all the time. I have no juices left inside me. Maybe you will fall ill yourself if you eat me, Ghachang Fu!"

"Forget Ghachang Fu," thundered the man. "Why did you clean up Guruji's pot of rosogollas in the train? Now the yogic serpents will take their revenge. If I hadn't slipped on a banana skin that day..."

My mouth fell open. My eyes became exactly like the rosogollas I had eaten.

"What? Then you are...you are..."

"Oh yes. I am Prabhuji's disciple, Gajeshwar Gadui."

"Wha...what?"

Gajeshwar smiled. "You thought you had got rid of us at Muri station. But we took the next train. Now you will learn your lesson."

My blood turned cold. Gajeshwar would surely make *shammi kebab* out of me. Okay, if I must die, I must. But let me understand these people before I die.

"But why are you people here? What do you need in Kyabla's uncle's bungalow? Why are you hiding in a hole in the mountain? And why have you kept a mound of rotten dung at the mouth of the hole?"

Gajeshwar was annoyed. "Why should we keep dung? A cow must have dropped it, maybe so that other cows like you slip on it."

"But why do you want us to leave? Why do you want this place to yourselves?"

"Why do you want to know all that, you shrimp?" Gajeshwar yawned.

I was furious. How dare he call me a shrimp? A red ant was biting on my right ear. I flicked it away and said, "Look, if you want to make chops or cutlets out of me, you may do so. But don't ever call me a shrimp."

"Why not? I will call you a shrimp if I want," smiled Gajeshwar.

"Never! Do you know, I sat for the School Final Exam twice?"

"Oh! School final!" said Gajeshwar, taking out a cigarette from his pocket. "So tell me, what is the meaning of 'cataclysm'?"

"Cataclysm?" I scratched my nose. "Is it another word for a kitten?"

"Wrong! Now, what is the capital of Semigembia?"

"Must be Honolulu. Or is it Madagascar?"

"I can see how you've massacred geography. Now tell me, what is the meaning of *aniket*?"

"Who Animesh? Animesh is my cousin."

"Enough, enough, don't try to show off your education," Gajeshwar scowled again like an owl. "You are so bad, you seem really quite inedible. Maybe I could cook you with a bit of bitter gourd. Now get up."

"Where are we going?"

"To the cold storage, of course! You will meet your friend Habul Sen there."

I started looking this way and that. In times of danger, even Pyalaram's brains start working. I tried to assess where I was. So far as I could see, I was inside a deep hole on a hill. If I had not fallen on Gajeshwar, I would have really hurt myself. The hole proceeded like a tunnel and the cold storage must be at its end. Habul Sen was lying there now.

But could I escape from here? Never.

I could see the round opening, like the mouth of a well, through which I had fallen. I noticed that the stones by the side of the well were uneven. I might just be able to climb up.

"Thinking of escaping, are you?" Gajeshwar looked at me with gleaming eyes. "Forget it! You can escape from a tiger's den, perhaps, but not from Gajeshwar. On top of that, you have torn off Gurudev's beard. God alone knows what is in store for you."

God! That tobacco-stained, demonic beard was then Swami Ghutghutananda's! He was probably eavesdropping, hidden in the bush, and I took that heavenly beard to be a squirrel's tail!

"Please!" I pleaded, "I thought..."

"I don't want to know what you thought. Gurudev screamed in pain for two hours. When he returns..., now come on!"

Gajeshwar stretched out a long arm like an elephant's trunk. Suddenly he cried out, "Help! Help! I am gone!"

I immediately saw what had happened. A black, vicious-looking scorpion was lying at Gajeshwar's feet, its claws still in the air.

"Oh Baba, I'm gone, I'm gone..."

The large man was writhing on the floor in pain. And I? I was not one to lose such a golden opportunity. I leapt on the first groove in the stone. Now, do or die!

Sheth Dhunduram

Up, up! Come on, climb up fast!

When I heaved myself out of the hole at last, my spleen was dancing like a giant turtle inside my belly. Not that I have ever seen a turtle dance. But if a turtle ever danced with joy, it would surely have jigged away, as my spleen was doing now. And it did not stop dancing for a full five minutes.

After my spleen quietened down, I held on to a branch of the kamranga tree and looked around. I could see no one. Who knew where Kyabla and Teni had gone? All I could see was a monkey sitting on an *amrul* tree opposite, making faces at me. I too stuck out my tongue and made a horrible face at him. He looked furious and disappeared among the leaves.

I could still hear Gajeshwar's groans rising from the hole. I felt happier. How dare he plan to make a cutlet out of me? Or ask the meanings of all those awful English words and the capital of Honolulu? That scorpion's sting would surely make him sing a different tune. Suddenly, my eyes felt upon that blasted lump of dung. The mark of my foot was still there. That lump was the reason of my fall. Furious, I gave it a kick.

Oh, oh, what was that? I got sprayed all over by the dung. What a badly-behaved lump of dung that was! No, I refused to stay there any more. What if Gajeshwar climbed up from the hole?

But which way to go? I knew I was somewhere behind the bungalow, but my directions had become like knotted noodles after the fall. Should I go left or right?

You know, I have this bad habit. Once out of Patoldanga, my sense of direction goes haywire. Once, at Deoghar, I told my cousin Fuchu, "Look Fuchu, how amazing! The sun is rising in the north!" Fuchu boxed my ears and said, "Go straight to Ranchi from here, Pyala. I mean, to Ranchi's asylum."

I was still thinking which way to go, when I suddenly caught my breath. Who were those people coming this way through the forest? Whose beard was dancing in the wind, like a squirrel's tail?

Surely it was Swami Ghutghutananda! And there were two hefty young men behind him, carrying earthen pots. Surely the pots had yogic serpents inside, that is, rosogollas. Habul Sen would get his share, undoubtedly!

I, Pyalaram of Patoldanga, had a real weakness for rosogollas. But even my love of sweets will not make me fall into Gajeshwar's clutches again. No, never!

I dived into the bushes to my left. I could not run, they would hear my footsteps. So I crept through the bushes.

I didn't know which way I was going, but I kept walking. I crossed bushes, leapt over ditches and nearly fell over a jackal. But I did not stop. I simply did not wish to face Bandit Ghachang Fu again. Gajeshwar would surely make bitter gourd curry out of me if he caught me again!

I walked at random for nearly an hour. Then I saw a small stream in front of me. The blue water was flowing over the loose sand. Big and small stones were scattered all around. My legs were collapsing under me, and my throat was completely dry.

I sat for a while on a stone. The place was cool and shady. Soon I felt better. There were palash trees on all sides. Two blue birds were playing on the other side of the stream.

I drank a little water from the stream. It was cool and sweet. I felt soothed and refreshed once again. I felt so good that I forgot all about Ghachang Fu, Gajeshwar, Teni, Kyabla and Habul Sen. *Cha-ra-ra-ra Rama ho, Rama ho...* I wanted to sing.

I had just begun, *Cha-ra-ra-ra,* when I heard a 'honk honk' from behind me.

The interruption really spoilt my mood! But how did a car appear in this jungle in the Jhanto Hills?

I now noticed a road running by the stream. And on that road, under the palash trees, was a blue motor car.

What if those people belonged to the Ghachang Fu gang? Wasn't this what we always read in detective stories–a dense forest, a car, three men in black masks, carrying pistols?

My malarial spleen started its turtle dance once again. I was just thinking of running away, when the horn sounded again: honk, honk! And then someone got down from the car.

At the sight of him, I stopped in my tracks. Surely no bandit gang could have a man like that? No detective story had ever featured such a figure.

It was a figure no crane could lift. He had the greatest pot belly I had ever seen. The silk kurta he wore must have been made from an entire roll of cloth. His face was like a bloated balloon, on his head he wore a huge yellow turban. He didn't seem to have a neck, and his head jutted straight out of his belly. A gold chain sparkled right under his chin, and he had ten gold rings on his ten fingers.

A perfect Sheth! No, he could not be a member of the Ghachang Fu gang. Just the opposite. He seemed to be a likely target of such gangs. But what was such a perfect Sheth doing in a forest?

"Boy! Hey you!"

The Sheth must be calling me, for I could not see any other boy around. I walked towards him.

"Namaste Shethji!"

"Namaste my child," the Sheth seemed to smile. I could see a few teeth and two twinkling eyes flashing from the balloon. He asked, "Whose son are you? What are you doing here?"

Should I tell him the truth? I decided not to. Jhanto Hills was not a nice place at all. Who knew what secrets the Sheth was hiding in his huge paunch?

"I am a student of a school in Hazaribagh," I lied. "We have come here for a picnic."

"What? For a picnic?" the Sheth's eyes twinkled once again from inside the balloon. "This far? And where are the other boys?"

"Must have gone that side," I pointed somewhere in the forest. Then I asked, "But who are you? What are you doing here?"

"Me? I am Sheth Dhunduram. I have a shop in Calcutta, and one at Ranchi. I have come here to lease the forest."

I suddenly felt like having fun at his expense. "But Shethji, don't roam too much in this jungle. We've heard that some bears are prowling around."

"What? Bears?" Sheth Dhunduram's large paunch jumped with fright. "Are they biting men?"

"Oh yes. Whenever they get a man, they bite."

"What?"

I assured the Sheth, "They are especially biting men with big paunches. Bears love paunches, you know!"

"Ram! Ram!" The Sheth suddenly jumped. If I hadn't seen him in action, I would never have believed that such a huge man could jump so high.

The four-ton figure in the silk sack ran to the car. "Hey, Chagan Lal, start the car! Quick!" he shouted.

Honk! Honk! In a second Dhunduram's blue car had vanished in the jungle. And for a full five minutes, I stood there and laughed. What a wonderful joke!

But not for long. Suddenly, from behind me, I heard a huge roar. 'Grrrrr!'

A tiger!

Now the joke was on me. I jumped higher than the Sheth...

And landed in the icy river. Once again, the roar came from behind me, 'Grrr!'

The Tiger Episode

How cold the water was! Even my bones were shivering with cold. The current was equally strong. It dragged me several feet in a few minutes.

But better stand in cold water than become a tiger's breakfast. I crossed the river, tripped on a stone and landed again in the water and swallowed a mouthful. The tiger would jump on me any minute.

And at that moment...

No, not a tiger's roar! It was a roar of laughter.

A tiger laughing! Could a tiger laugh? I had seen many tigers in the zoo, but I have never heard one laughing. I have thought a lot about tigers. Do tigers snore when they sleep? What do their snores sound like?

Once, to hear a tiger sneeze, I had taken along a packet of snuff. Just as I was aiming it at the tiger, my cousin Fuchu snatched the packet from my hands and boxed my ears.

But did I ever dream I would hear a tiger's laughter?

Once again I tripped on a stone and fell in the water. Again that roar of laughter, and then someone said,

"Come out of the water, Pyala! You'll surely die of double pneumonia if you stay on!"

Who was that? Who else but Kyabla! And Teni was there too. Both were smiling, showing all their teeth.

Teni screwed up his long nose and said, "One tiger-call from behind, and you jumped into water! What a coward you are, Pyala!"

What a stupid joke! How dare they play those tricks on me, drenching me this early in the morning! I came out of the river, fuming. "What's the meaning of this?" I asked.

Kyabla replied, "We were about to ask you that, Pyala. You were coming behind us, then you vanished into thin air. We spent hours looking for you. At last we found you sitting here, laughing like a mad man. So we too had a little laugh at your expense!"

"I fell into Ghachang Fu's den," I replied.

"What?" they both stared, open-mouthed.

"Or Swami Ghutghutananda's den, if you like."

"Swami Ghutghutananda?" Kyabla gulped. Teni stood there, his mouth open, like a thirsty crow.

"And with him is Gajeshwar Gadui, that elephant-like man," I added.

"What?"

"And then there is Sheth Dhunduram's blue car."

"What?"

They were stunned. I was really enjoying myself. Should I start the song again? I thought better of it. I was so cold! I knew all that would come out of my voice would be classical *taans*. "Let's get back to the bungalow," I said, "then I will tell you all about it."

When I told them the whole story, they refused to believe me. "Swami Ghutghutananda is Ghachang Fu! And Gajeshwar Gadui is with him! And they are living in a hole in the hill? Come on Pyala, stop joking!"

Teni said, "Surely he had fever while wandering in the forest, and dreamt these fantastic things in a feverish sleep."

"Feverish sleep, is it?" I said. "Fine, you'll see Gajeshwar Gadui soon enough, as soon as the sting of the scorpion hurts a little less. You are our leader. He will make fowl cutlet out of you!"

"Fowl means chicken," said Kyabla. "Tenida can't be a chicken because he doesn't have wings. Perhaps one can make mutton cutlet out of him. But lambs have four legs. Tenida, can your hands be called legs?"

Teni tried to slap Kyabla. Kyabla dodged and his hand fell on the back of a chair. "Oooh" cried Teni and started dancing in pain.

After a while, when his dance was over, Teni said, "It is my fault. I should not have brought a couple of idiots along with me. God knows where Habul is. How can I manage so many things at once?"

"Manage? You managing us?" said Kyabla. "By now we know what kind of leader you are! You yourself need to be managed all the while."

Teni was again about to slap Kyabla, but again Kyabla dived off the chair.

I became angry. "You people are wasting time like this. By now Gajeshwar might have made a chop out of Habul."

"Mutton chop," said Kyabla. "That Habul is no better than a sheep. But let's go Tenida, we must find out whether Pyala is telling the truth. Come on Pyala, show us where your Ghutghutananda's den is. Get up, Tenida."

"Wait," said Teni, scratching his nose. "Let me think."

"What's there to think about?" said Kyabla. "Ready? Quick march! One, two, three!"

Teni made a face as if he had taken quinine pills. "Er, I was saying, should we jump into the enemy's den like this? We only have a few sticks, they may have pistols and guns. Besides, we don't know how many they are, and we are only three. Even Jhantu has gone to the bazaar..."

Kyabla stuck out his breast. "What can happen, Tenida? At the worst, they will kill us. It is better to die like heroes than to live like cowards. Should we, the boys of Patoldanga, leave our friend at the mercy of those goons and escape?"

Believe me, looking at those bright eyes of Kyabla, I too suddenly felt an upsurge of courage. Better die like a hero than live on like a mouse. Besides, a man only dies once!

I looked up and found that Teni, too, was standing upright. Not the hesitant, scared Teni, but the champion of Patoldanga. Now he gave out a roar, "Right you are, Kyabla! You have brought me back to my senses. Either we take Habul Sen with us back to Calcutta, or we give up our lives."

The leader was speaking at last!

All three of us went out at once. They had their sticks. I had lost my piece of wood somewhere, so I had to find another piece. This time it was not difficult to spot the place.

There was the kamranga tree, then the lump of dung, which had made me slip. But the hole? Where was the hole?

There was no sign of the hole. In its place was a bush.

"Where is your hole?" said Kyabla.

"Well ..."

"Didn't I tell you he was dreaming? How can Swami Ghutghutananda be Ghachang Fu?"

My head started reeling. Did I really imagine all that in a dream brought on by fever? But then, how could I still feel that pain all over my body? The mark of my foot was still there on the pile of dung. Then how could that large hole vanish?

"Your hole has run away at the sight of us, Pyala," said Teni with a mocking smile. And kicked at the bush.

Immediately the bush shook, as if in an earthquake. Teni shook it even more. Then he vanished along with the bush, like Sita being swallowed up by the earth. Thud! came a sound from inside.

Those were not bushes. Someone had cut branches from trees and hidden the mouth of the hole.

Kyabla and I stood there. We didn't know what to do.

Then we heard Teni's voice, "Kyabla! Pyala!"

"What's happened, Tenida?" we cried.

"I'm just a little hurt, nothing much. Both of you come down here. Put your feet in the grooves. You won't believe what's happening here!"

The hair on my hands stood on end. Do or die, I told myself once again. And stepped into the hole, climbing down. Kyabla was close behind me.

Habul sen's Body

Kyabla and I climbed down. But we could see no one. No Teni, no Gajeshwar, not even a hair of Swami Ghutghutananda's beard.

Had the gang of Ghachang Fu vanished Teni too?

Kyabla looked at me and said, "Teni fell right here. Where can he have gone?"

I was looking out for that scorpion all the time. That huge Gajeshwar might have survived its sting, but I surely will not!

Kyabla gave me a shove. "Hey, where is Tenida?"

"How do I know?"

"Strange!" said Kyabla, "He can't vanish into thin air."

But Teni, our great leader, was not one to vanish so

easily. Again we heard his voice, "Kyabla, Pyala! Come down here. This is terrible!"

But where was he? Where should we go? My hair stood on end. "Where are you, Tenida?" shouted Kyabla. "We can't see you at all!"

Again Teni's voice came, "I'm downstairs!"

"What do you mean, downstairs?"

Now Teni sounded furious. "Are you blind? Can't you see the hole in front of you?"

He was right! There was a big hole in the stone wall. We went near it and saw a bamboo ladder. Deep mystery indeed!

"Climb down," ordered Teni. "Look what a horrible thing has happened."

Kyabla went down, I followed him. The place was like a large hall. Light filtered down from somewhere. We could clearly see an earthen *chula*, a few broken pots and pans, and on one side...

A heap of ashes! And on it lay Habul Sen.

"Why is Habul lying there like that?" I whispered.

Teni's voice was shaking. "He must have been murdered," he said.

I don't know what fear does to you, but I felt as if I was turning into a turtle. My hands and feet were sinking inside my belly. I felt a hard cover form over my back. Perhaps I would start creeping towards water in a moment?

All I could mumble was, "That is Habul's body!"

Teni suddenly started howling. "Oh, oh, Habul! Why did you die like this? What will I tell your granny when we go back to Calcutta? Oh, oh, who will treat me to sweets and chaat like you did?"

"Stop crying," said Kyabla. "Let us first see whether he is alive or not."

I too felt like crying. Habul would often steal mango and plum pickle from his granny's storeroom and give them to me. Sheer gratitude brought tears to my eyes. I rubbed my nose with the end of my dhoti.

I sniffed and said, "Surely he is dead. Otherwise, why is he lying like that?"

Kyabla crept forward, and gave Habul's body a shove. And at once–how strange–Habul Sen sat up!

"A ghost!" I cried and jumped. And at once bumped against Teni's nose. What a hard nose! I thought my head was punctured.

"My nose! My nose!" cried Teni, and I fell to the ground.

And at that moment, Habul Sen said, loud and clear, "I was having such a marvellous sleep after a pot of rosogollas! Now you have spoilt it all." He certainly did not sound like a ghost!

Teni began to scold him, "Oh yes, haven't you found a royal bed at last? You idiot, here you are sleeping like a Nawab, and we have been going round and round madly, searching for you. Have you got no sense?"

Habul yawned. "Hmmm," he said, "the rosogollas had brought on such a magnificent sleep. But where is Swamiji? And Gajada?"

"Aha! So Gajeshwar has become your Gajada now?" cried Teni.

"Why not?" replied Habul. "Look how well they have treated me! I arrived here yesterday evening, and since then they have been stuffing me with food. But where have they gone?"

"How can we possibly know where they have disappeared?" said Kyabla. "But how did you come here?"

"A man came and told me, 'There is treasure underneath this hill. Would you like to take it?' I didn't want to lose this chance. So I came here. And Swamiji and Gajada were so nice to me!"

"Here you sat eating rosogollas, and there we were scared out of our wits," grumbled Teni.

"Enough," said Kyabla. "Tell us, Habul, how many of them live in this hole?"

"About four of them."

"What did they do?"

"How do I know? But there was a machine, and the men were printing something in it. I can't see the machine either. Have they left forever?" A deep sigh came out of Habul's throat.

"Now let's get out of here," said Teni. "Thank God we came just in time. Otherwise they would have killed you by making you overeat."

"No, no," I said. "They would have fattened you and made cutlets out of you."

"Will you stop speaking nonsense?" said Kyabla. "Listen Habul, did you see what they printed?"

"Something with pictures," was all Habul could say.

"Pictures?" Kyabla scratched his nose. "Printing something with pictures in a hole in the hills. Trying to evict people staying in the bungalow. A blue car in the forest. Sheth Dhunduram. What does all this mean?"

"Forget about Sheth Dhunduram," said Teni. "We have found Habul, the adventure is over. He might have eaten rosogollas, but we haven't had anything since morning. Can you imagine what's happening inside my belly? Let's get out of here."

"Climb up that ladder again?" I whined.

"Why the ladder?" said Habul. "We can get out this way."

"Which way?"

Habul showed us. We crossed the tunnel-like hall and wow! There was an opening was right before us, near the river and the saal forest.

"But Habul, you could have easily escaped!" said Kyabla.

"Why should I?" said Habul. "I thought I'd stay here for a while, improve my health a bit."

"You greedy goat," shouted Teni. "If Gajeshwar had made cutlets out of you, it would have served you right."

Right then, we heard the roar of a car.

Was that Sheth Dhunduram again?

Yes, it was. That same blue car. But it wasn't coming this side. It was disappearing fast into the jungle, as if running away from us.

And I saw clearly that a beard was flying from inside the car. A tobacco-stained, white beard.

Swami Ghutghutananda's beard?

The Bird has Fled

Kyabla watched Sheth Dhunduram's blue car disappear and said, "Chuk-chuk-chu."

"What is it, Kyabla?" asked Teni.

"The bird has fled," said Kyabla.

"What bird? I can see two crows sitting over there," I offered helpfully.

"You idiot, Pyala," cried Kyabla. "Didn't you see all of them escape in Sheth Dhunduram's car? Didn't you see Swami Ghutghutananda's beard?"

Teni said, "I am glad those troublemakers are gone."

Habul was still sleepy. The effect of the rosogollas hadn't worn off. Suddenly he opened his eyes like an owl and said, "Oh, has Gajada left? What a nice man, Gajada."

"Shut up Habul," said Kyabla. "Nice man indeed! So nice that he wants to force us out of the bungalow, and print something sitting in a hole in the hills. And why do you think Dhunduram goes around in the forest in a blue car? Hmm, I think I've got it!"

"What have you understood from all this?" asked Teni.

Kyabla did not answer him. He turned round and looked at us with blazing eyes. Then he asked in a deep voice, "Who are the cowards in our team?"

The way he said these words made my tummy rumble. Once, on the day of a maths test, I was lying down, pretending I had a stomach ache. My brother, who was then a medical student, came with a long syringe. At the sight of it, my ache vanished. Looking at Kyabla, I now felt that he was chasing me with such a syringe.

I was about to say that I was the only coward, when I checked myself.

"No cowards," said Teni. "We are all brave."

"Then let us go."

"Where?"

"We will have to catch that blue car."

Was he mad? Did he think the car was like Ghutghutananda's beard, that we could reach out and grab it with our hands?

"How are we going to catch the car? We can't fly, can we?" said Habul.

"Let's go to the main road. A lot of trucks run there, and they will surely give us a ride if we give them some money."

"And do you suppose the blue car will wait for us till then?"

"Where can the car go? Ramgarh, at the most. We will catch them if we reach Ramgarh."

"What if we don't?"

"Then we will come back."

"But why take all this trouble?" said Teni. "Let them escape. Now we can go back to the bungalow and make good use of the chicken legs Jhantu has cooked for us. Those terrible laughs won't wake us up in the night anymore."

"Never," said Kyabla, thumping his own chest. "They have escaped, making us look like fools. If we don't catch them, we are not fit to live in Patoldanga! If you people don't come, I am going alone."

"Alone?" said Teni.

"Yes, alone."

Teni let out a long sigh. "Okay then, let's all go together."

I scratched my head for the last time. "But Gajeshwar is with them," I said. "That time he was floored by the scorpion. If he catches us again, he will surely make cutlets out of all of us. Or maybe curry with onions. Or *vadas*."

Kyabla made a face at me. "Fine then, you stay here," he said. "We are leaving."

I saw them leaving in a single file. Without me. So I had to run after them. The main road was about one and a half miles away from our bungalow. We could see the car track running through the forest. At one place, I saw a saal leaf plate lying on the road. Feeling curious, I picked it up and smelled it. How it smelled of samosas!

But those people had finished off all the samosas! Inconsiderate beasts!

"Hey Pyala, why have you stopped in the middle of the road?" Teni shouted.

They couldn't even bear my smelling the packet. I had to throw it away and follow them once again. I felt so bad! I really had wanted to smell the packet some more.

We reached the main road. Honk! honk! A lorry was coming our way. I was about to stop the lorry but Kyabla stopped me.

"What are you doing? That one is coming from Ramgarh!"

"Maybe they have gone the other way."

"Don't be a silly billy. Can't you see how the wheels

have taken a turn on the *kutcha* road? They have gone to Ramgarh, not to Hazaribagh."

Really, how intelligent Kyabla was! That was why he stood first in all exams, and all I got was a string of zeros!

Ghrrr-ghsshh!

A lorry stopped before us. It was loaded with wood. The driver stuck out his neck and said, "What are you doing here, boys?"

"Will you drop us at Ramgarh?"

"That will be four annas each."

"No problem."

"Come up, then. But you will have to sit on the wood."

"That's fine."

Kyabla pushed us. "Come on, get up. Habul, what are you doing? Why are you standing there, Pyala? Get up, quick!"

They got up on to the lorry. But it was not an easy task for me. My belly got scraped, and my whole body burnt.

At once, the lorry started on the road to Ramgarh. How the pieces of wood jumped! I felt I'd be thrown off the lorry. I lay face down and held on to a huge tree trunk.

The lorry ran in full speed. I felt as if my insides were crying out in chorus.

The Lethal Ladder

How the lorry ran! And how the logs of wood danced! Though they were tied firmly with thick rope, I felt as if they would scatter all around, and me with them.

Have you seen berries being shaken? Small, plump, black berries are put in two bowls, the mouth of the two bowls are held together and then shaken vigorously, till the seeds and the pulp fall apart. I felt as if my condition would soon be like those berries. "I won't remain Pyalaram of Patoldanga for long. I will soon become a tortoise of Vrindavan," I thought.

On top of this, the branch of a tree whipped us on our heads.

"All because of Kyabla. We will now die in this wilderness," said Teni.

That stupid Kyabla tried to joke. "Not in the wilderness, but on the way to Ramgarh!"

"On the way!" mimicked Teni. "Wait till we reach Ramgarh. Then I'll–gulp!"

He did not mean he would gulp down Kyabla. That sound was forced out of him by another big jerk.

Habul started complaining. "The rosogollas Gajada fed me so lovingly have all turned to *paneer.*"

"Now the paneer will turn to milk," I replied.

"Milk? Do you think it will stop there?" added Teni. "Just wait till a whole cow, horns and all, comes out of your belly."

Kyabla started singing, "*O Nataraj, when you started your dance of destruction ...*"

Teni was about to shout something, when another big jerk silenced him again.

But all sorrows come to an end. The lorry reached Ramgarh bazaar at last. It was moving slowly. Suddenly...

"Hey Bhaglu, look! Four boys sitting on top of the lorry like monkeys!"

Three boys were laughing at us. I was furious. "Monkey yourself. Idiots!" I shouted. At once, one of them threw a stone at us. It narrowly missed my ear. The driver shouted, "I'll pull off all your hair!"

The boys stuck out their tongues at us and vanished somewhere.

The lorry went ahead a little farther when Kyabla said, "Tenida, quick! There's the blue car!"

He was right! Sheth Dhunduram's blue car was standing in front of a sweet shop.

My heart starting thumping. Must I face Gajeshwar again? Why not stay on top of the logs like a tortoise?

But Kyabla was not one to let us go. He dragged us down.

"Listen Pyala, Habul and you sit under this peepul tree and watch that blue car. Tenida and I will be back soon."

The lorry driver had taken his money and left. If the lorry had been anywhere near, I would have jumped upon it and gone wherever it was going. What a mess! What if Gajeshwar came and attacked me while I watched the car?

"Can't I come with you?" I said. "Habul can keep watch alone!"

"Do what we say," said Kyabla. "Watch the car. We will be back in ten minutes. Come Tenida." The two of them vanished through a side street.

"Habul!" I called.

"Hmmm?" he said.

"Just look at what they did. Why should we sit here like fools?"

Habul yawned and said, "Right, why sit? Let's lie down here and go to sleep. You people woke me up, and then there was that journey on the lorry! I am aching all over!"

Habul sat with his back against the peepul tree and shut his eyes. And soon, believe me, he started snoring!

"Habul! Habul!" I called.

His nose stopped singing. "Hmmm?" he said.

"How can you sleep under a tree, in broad daylight?"

Habul made a face and said, "Look Pyala, don't disturb me. Let me sleep in peace." And immediately he went off to sleep again. His nose made a sound as if a whole group of sparrows were flying out of it.

I can't tell you how angry I was! Was I supposed to keep a watch on him as well? I thought of pinching his ears. But no, there should be a better way of waking him up. Some fat, big red ants were marching at the bottom of the tree. Should I place a few of them on Habul's nose?

I was about to pick up a dry leaf to catch a few red ants when ...

"Hello, young boy? How come you are here?"

It was Sheth Dhunduram!

My insides started jumping with fear. My mouth fell open. All that escaped was, "I...I..."

"So you are visiting Ramgarh? Good, good. But why are you sitting here? You look hungry, too."

Hungry? What was he saying? Since I smelled that plate of samosas, I had felt like howling. I felt I could eat anything that came my way. In fact, I could happily take a bite of Sheth Dhunduram's big paunch. But how could one say that?

Sheth Dhunduram said, "Why are you feeling shy? Come with me. That shop over there sells nice *laddus*, and hot samosas too. I will treat you, you don't have to pay."

Pyalaram of Patoldanga did not fear tigers, or even Teni's slaps. Nor could a zero in maths make me tremble. But once someone mentioned food, your heroic Pyalaram was done for.

"B-but Shethji, Gajeshwar..." I stammered.

"Gajeshwar? Who's he?" the Sheth raised his eyebrows.

"That man the size of an elephant, who has come with you in your car..."

"Ram Ram," said Dhunduram. "I don't know any Gajeshwar. I have come alone in my car."

"But we saw Ghutghutananda's beard!"

"Ghutghutananda?" Dhunduram thought for a while. "Oh yes, an old man did take a lift in my car. He requested me to drop him at Ramgarh bazaar. I've dropped him, he has gone to the station."

After this, why should I disbelieve him?

Dhunduram said, "Come on, samosas, laddus..."

Patoldanga's Pyalaram could not resist any more. Sparrows were still fluttering inside Habul's nose. Should I wake him up? No, I thought, let him sleep. I followed Dhunduram to the shop.

It was a big shop. Laddus and *motichurs* were displayed in a heap. A man was frying samosas in a big *kadai*. The smell made me feel faint.

"Come in, come in," said the Sheth.

I looked everywhere. No trace of Gajeshwar or Ghutghutananda. I stepped in.

There was a small eating place inside the shop. Shethji sat down and ordered, "One dozen special laddus and six samosas."

"Why so many, Shethji?" I wanted to be polite.

"Aarey, young man, eat well," smiled the Shethji.

The laddus and samosas came on a saal leaf. I tasted the laddus. Wonderful! I took a bite of the samosa. Terrific! I got down to work. I had eaten about four laddus and two samosas, when suddenly my head started reeling. Then everything turned dark before my eyes. And then...

I heard Gajeshwar's roar of laughter.

"Got him at last! The imp! Now I'll make aalu chaat out of him."

The whole world became dark. I fell, chair and all, on the floor.

The End Of the Tale

"Where am I?"

That was my first thought when I woke up. And when I looked around, I could not believe my eyes.

Not Jhanto Hills. Not Ramgarh. I was near the peak of a large hill. The peak was like an oven. Flames of fire were coming up from it. I knew what it was. I had read about it in geography books. I had seen it in films too. "This must be a volcano," I said.

Immediately there rose a terrible laughter. 'Ha ha ha' it went, till the whole hill started shaking with the sound. A large flame leapt up from the crater.

I found three men rolling on the ground with laughter. One was Sheth Dhunduram, his paunch dancing like waves as he laughed. Beside him was Ghutghutananda, pulling his own beard as he laughed. And leaning against the hill was the gigantic Gajeshwar—his mouth opened wide enough to swallow the whole world—letting out roars of laughter.

Looking at the three of them, I almost died of fright. My insides started quivering.

"Why are you laughing so much?" I asked, scared.

Once again they laughed. Gajeshwar clutched his stomach and sat down.

"Ho, ho," replied Dhunduram, "This is a volcano, to be sure! Do you know which volcano it is?"

"How do I know? I have never seen one before."

"This is the Vesuvius," he said.

"Vesuvius?" I gulped. I did not know that Vesuvius was so close to Ramgarh!

"Isn't the Vesuvius in Germany? Or is that Africa?"

Gajeshwar made a face at me. "Phoo!" he said, "And are you talking of passing the school final exam! The Vesuvius is in Germany? In Africa?"

"Is it in America, then?"

Gajeshwar said, "No, I can see you have only dung in your head. No wonder you get zero in exams. The Vesuvius is in Italy."

"Is it?" I said. "Well, Italy and America are the same thing, really."

"The same thing!" exclaimed Gajeshwar. "Are your head

and your legs the same thing? Are mutton curry and vegetable kofta the same?"

"Never mind what he says," said Ghutghutananda. "His head is really not different from his legs. There is nothing inside that head of his."

I was angry. "Okay, what's your problem? All I want to know is, how did I come to Italy from Ramgarh? And when? Where are Teni, Habul and Kyabla? I can't see any of them."

"You'll never see them again," smiled Gajeshwar. "We have eaten them up. They are pretty well digested by now."

"Eaten them up?" I shouted, my malarial spleen jumping to my throat. Once again the three laughed in chorus. The sound made flames leap up again from the mouth of the Vesuvius. I covered my ears with my hands.

At last, Ghutghutananda stopped laughing and said, "How could you tiny things dare to fight against us? Now you know what happens if a sheep tries to fight with a Royal Bengal Tiger. With my yogic power, I brought all four of you here. And then..."

Shethji said, "We roasted Habul Sen..."

Gajeshwar said, "We made cutlets of your leader Teni..."

Swamiji said, "We fried that talkative boy, Kyabla..."

"...And we ate them up," finished Shethji.

My hair stood on end. I gulped thrice and said, "What?"

"Now it's your turn," said Swamiji. "Gajeshwar!"

"Yes, Maharaj," said Gajeshwar, with folded hands.

"Put on the kadai."

At once Gajeshwar took out a kadai from somewhere. What a kadai! It looked like a huge boat. All four of us could be made into a curry in it.

"Put it on the fire," ordered Swamiji.

Gajeshwar climbed to the peak of the Vesuvius and put the kadai on the crater. "Is there enough oil?" asked Swamiji.

"Oh yes," said Gajeshwar, "Pure oil."

"It's from my own oil mill, Prabhu," said Sheth Dhunduram.

"Good, good," said the Swami. "Impure oil does not suit my stomach. It causes acidity."

I could not keep quiet any more. "What will you do with pure oil?" I howled.

"We will fry you," replied Gajeshwar Gadui.

Swamiji said, "And then, with some fresh muri..."

"...We will munch you up," finished the Shethji.

So the end had come for Pyalaram of Patoldanga. Now he would be digested inside the stomachs of these three demons. Suddenly, I felt all fear leaving me. A heavenly calm descended upon me. Do you know how this happens? Suppose you have sat down for an exam. You find that none of the sums are clear to you. For some time, you sweat. Crickets buzz inside your ears, a fly dances around your nose. Then suddenly, you find yourself calming down. You start drawing a coconut tree in your copy. And hills behind it, the moon, birds flying, and so on. That is, you give up all hope and become an artist.

So when I found there was no hope for me, I felt like singing a song. All my life I have never really sung a song. At home, my elder brother chases me with his fat medical books if I try to sing. Outside, Teni silences me with a slap. Now I wanted to sing a song for the last time. I would never get a chance to sing again.

I said, "Prabhu! Swamiji!"

Swamiji said, "What is you wish? Should we fry you dipped in batter, or with just salt and turmeric?"

"Whichever way you want," I said. "I have only one request. I want to sing one last song before I die."

"Not a bad idea," said Gajeshwar. "A little music before dinner will be fine. Africans, too, sing and dance before they eat up men. Start!"

"Yes, yes," said Shethji. "Sing us a nice song."

I closed my eyes and began:

> *Once a bone got stuck,*
> *In a tiger's throat,*
> *Try as he might the bone*
> *Would not come out.*

"What's this?" said Shethji. "This is a fable, not a song!"

"Let him sing," said Swamiji. "What a voice he has, just like an owl's. Go on, go on."

I kept my eyes closed and sang on:

Boo-hoo cried the tiger
Mad with the pain,
Till at last the tiger ran
To his friend, the crane...

I had sung till here, when I suddenly heard a sound: Jhum! Jhum! It was as if someone was dancing. I opened my eyes and found Gajeshwar dancing.

Yes, it was Gajeshwar. He was wearing a *ghagra*, a nose ring on his nose, *ghungroo* on his feet, and now he was dancing round and round, like a peacock. I don't know if the Tadaka *rakshashi* of Ramayana ever danced in a ghagra. Even if she did, she could never hold a candle to Gajeshwar.

Gajeshwar saw me staring at him. He smiled and said, "What are you staring at? Could your Udayshankar ever dance like this? Huh? This is pure *Kathakali.*"

"You could call it *Manipuri* too," said Swamiji.

"Or even *Kathak*," added the Shethji.

"Or *Tadaka* dance," I said.

"What did you say?" said Gajeshwar.

"Oh, nothing, nothing," I said hastily.

"Yes, you keep quiet," Gajeshwar swished his ghagra around. "Why have you stopped singing? Come on, start! Let me dance to my heart's content!"

But Gajeshwar's dance had stopped my song half-way. It just would not come out.

"Phoo! You hardly know how to sing. Listen to me. I will sing you a classical song while I dance."

And Gajeshwar started singing:

Now Kali, I'll eat you up,

Hmm, hmm, eat you up, eat you up.

I'll snatch your garland made of heads, hmm hmm,

And cook you with ketchup.

And once again he started dancing. How he danced. It felt as if the entire Vesuvius was dancing with him.

The Swamiji and the Sheth were absorbed in the music and dance.

A voice spoke inside me, "This is your last chance. Run!"

I jumped up. And I started running with all my might.

But it was impossible to run fast on the Vesuvius. I tripped on a stone and fell. And immediately...

Gajeshwar stopped his dance. And stretching out a twenty-mile long arm, he caught me.

"How dare you escape while I am dancing. Now you'll know..."

So saying, he caught hold of my neck, lifted me into the air, and...

"Jai Guru Ghutghutananda!" he shouted, and threw me into that kadai of boiling oil...

No, not boiling oil. In ice cold water. I sat up, gulping. What was this? I felt as if I could still see the Vesuvius, Gajeshwar's dance, the huge kadai, before my eyes.

"Must have given him some drug," said a deep voice.

I looked up and saw a police officer twirling his moustache. With him were some constables and behind them, tied together with a rope...Swami Ghutghutananda, Sheth Dhunduram and Gajeshwar!

Teni was pouring water on my head, Habul was fanning me. And Kyabla was saying, "Get up, Pyala, get up. We had gone to the police station. The police have caught the whole gang. They were printing counterfeit notes beneath the hills. Swamiji was their leader. The Sheth used to launder the notes. They have found the printing machines in their car. The ghosts will not haunt the bungalow and Jhanto Hills any longer!"

The officer smiled and said, "Well done, boys. We were trying to catch this gang for quite some time, but could not get hold of them. Because of you, we could get them today. You will get a lot of money as reward from the government."

How could I keep sitting after that? I, Pyalaram of Patoldanga, leapt up. With all my lung power, I shouted, "Patoldanga..."

Teni, Habul Sen and Kyabla shouted together, "Zindabad!"